Dolcissimo

Dolcissimo

by

GIUSEPPE BONAVIRI

Translated from the Italian
with an introduction by
Umberto Mariani

ITALICA PRESS
NEW YORK
1990

Italian Copyright © 1978 by Rizzoli Editore, Milano

Translation Copyright © 1990 by Umberto Mariani

ITALICA PRESS, INC.
595 Main Street
New York, New York 10044

Library of Congress Cataloging-in-Publication Data

Bonaviri, Giuseppe, 1924-
   [Dolcissimo. English]
   Dolcissimo / by Giuseppe Bonaviri ; translated from the Italian with an introduction by Umberto Mariani.
      p.   cm.
   Translation of: Dolcissimo.
   ISBN 0-934977-21-6 : $12.50
   I. Title.
PQ4864.Q496D613   1990
853'.914--dc20   89-46224
                                      CIP

Printed in the United States of America
5 4 3 2 1

Cover photo by Norman F. Carver, Jr. from *Italian Hilltowns.*

Works of Giuseppe Bonaviri

Poetry

Il dire celeste (The language of the heavens). Rome: Editori Riuniti, 1976.

Il dire celeste e altre poesie (The language of the heavens and other poems). Milan: Guanda, 1979.

Nel silenzio della luna (In the silence of the moon). Sora: Edizioni dei Dioscuri, 1979.

Di fumo cilestrino (Of bluish smoke). Ancona: Dossier Arte, 1981.

Quark. Rome: Edizioni della Cometa, 1982.

O corpo sospiroso (O sighing body). Milan: Rizzoli, 1982.

Il re bambino (The baby king). Milan: Mondadori, 1990.

Prose-Poetry

L'incominciamento (Beginnings). Palermo: Sellerio, 1983.

Novels

Il sarto della stradalunga (The tailor of Main Street). Turin: Einaudi, 1954.

Il fiume di pietra (River of stone). Turin: Einaudi, 1964.

La divina foresta (The divine forest). Milan: Rizzoli, 1969.

Notti sull'altura (Highland nights). Milan: Rizzoli, 1971.

Le armi d'oro (Arms of gold). Milan: Rizzoli, 1973.

L'isola amorosa (The loving island). Milan: Rizzoli, 1973.

La Beffària (The big joke). Milan: Rizzoli, 1975.

Martedina. Rome: Editori Riuniti, 1976.

L'enorme tempo (A dreadful time). Milan: Rizzoli, 1976.

Dolcissimo. Milan: Rizzoli, 1978.

È un rosseggiar di peschi e d'albicocchi (Everywhere the rose of peach and apricot trees). Milan: Rizzoli, 1986.

Il dormiveglia (Between sleep and waking). Milan: Mondadori, 1988.

Ghigò. Milan: Mondadori, 1990.

Short Stories

La contrada degli ulivi (Where the olive trees grow). Venice: Sodalizio del Libro, 1958.

Il treno blu (The blue train). Florence: La Nuova Italia, 1978.

Novelle saracene (Saracen stories). Milan: Rizzoli, 1980.

Theater

Follia (Madness). Catania: Società di Storia Patria, 1976.

Criticism

L'arenario (The sandpit). Milan: Rizzoli, 1984.

About the Translator

Umberto Mariani was born in Italy in 1927. He received a doctorate in Italian literature from the University of Pavia in 1955 and an M.A. in American literature from New York University in 1959. Since then he has taught Italian literature at Rutgers University. His critical publications and translations include both American and Italian authors. Professor Mariani has been a coeditor of *Italian Quarterly* for several years and is also the editor of *NEMLA Italian Studies.*

INTRODUCTION

Readers new to the work of Giuseppe Bonaviri will find it useful to know that the author was born, in 1924, in the hilltop town of Mineo in Sicily. Not only because Mineo is actually the scene of all his books, even when the story is said to take place in India or on the plain of Troy or in intergalactic space, but also because of the powerful stimulus that, according to Bonaviri, Mineo exercises on the imagination of its inhabitants. Many of its simple peasants and artisans ventured on the mysterious paths of poetry; the author's father, Settimo Emanuele (Nané) Bonaviri (1902-1964), a tailor so shy he would go out of his way to avoid meeting in the street and thereby embarrassing a peasant who had not yet been able to pay him for a suit, secretly wrote poetry, which his son eventually edited as *L'arcano*. His mother, Giuseppina (Papé) Casaccio, youngest of the twenty-four children of the town's best baker at the turn of the century, was, like many of the women of Mineo, a gold mine of old tales and fables, who enthralled her wide-eyed children on winter nights with her superb skill as a storyteller and, in her eighties, set down her tales in small notebooks for her son, who reworked a number of them in his *Novelle saracene*.

Bonaviri maintains that the physical features of his native town were a powerful force in themselves, shaping his imagination and giving him a rich fund of memories on which his later work was to draw. Built on the crest of a hill in the ranges that rise from the plain of Catania, Mineo had a magnificent view of the hills and valleys to the east and the mountains of Central Sicily to the west, covered with flowers in spring and parched for the rest of the year; flights of bird infinite in number and variety passed over it; its winds blew constantly, now fierce, now gentle, bearing different odors, different voices in each season; its skies were deep and clear, everchanging and familiar, skies that were to be seen only before the age of industrial smog and sodium streetlighting.

Bonaviri began to write poems, stories, and novels before he was ten, and kept on writing through his high-school and university years in the nearby provincial capital, Catania, where he started medical school in 1943, receiving his degree in 1949. Many of his youthful works were later published in *Il treno blu, Di fumo cilestrino,* and *Quark.*

After getting his degree and while waiting to be drafted, he had begun work on a novel. The draft took him to the Military Academy in Florence in 1950 and to Alessandria and Casal Monferrato in Piedmont the following year, during which time he finished his novel. The well-known writer Elio Vittorini liked it and accepted it for publication in a series of new writers he was editing for the Turin publisher Einaudi. *Il sarto della stradalunga* (1954) is the story of the author's childhood, although the major figures are the members of his family, and particularly his father, the tailor of the title. In the post-war period when Neorealism dominated both literature and cinema, one wrote about Italy's recent tragedy, the poverty and suffering that accompanied Fascism, the war, the German occupation, the Resistance, and in a quasi-documentary style; anything else would have been considered heretical. But in Bonaviri's novel the starkly realistic elements of the material were subjected to the workings of a powerful imagination.

This was to be increasingly characteristic of all his later work, including the short stories of *La contrada degli ulivi* and his second novel, *Il fiume di pietra* (1962), which deals with the author's adolescence, with the passage of the front through his region in World War II, and with the end of Fascism. In the meantime, he spent several years as a doctor in Mineo, part of that time as the Public Health Officer, and he was often involved in fruitless struggles with the do-nothing attitude of the corrupt provincial and municipal governments – an experience later turned into fiction in *L'enorme tempo*. Bonaviri moved to the Ciociaria region, between Rome and Cassino, where he married in 1957 and where for a few years, as a member of the staff of the hospital of Frosinone, he experienced even greater frustration and anguish than in Mineo. Some of this experience too was translated into fiction, in the early chapters of *Martedina,* written in 1960. Since 1964, when he left the hospital for private practice as a cardiologist in Frosinone, he has been able to dedicate half of his time to writing.

A new literary direction began in 1969 with *La divina foresta*, the story of a molecule tossed through the winds of space, which finally finds, in the vicinity of Mineo, the propitious place for its later adventures, first as a plant and later as a hawk. *Notti sull'altura* concerns the family's search, following the death of the tailor of Main Street, for the "psychic remains" of their beloved and ultimately for the meaning of death. In *L'isola amorosa* the quest becomes an exploration of the restlessness and anguish of contemporary man. In *La*

Beffària peasant wisdom views the chaos and narrow materialism of our time satirically.

Most of the novels from *Martedina* to *Dolcissimo* (1978) are stories of quest, transformation, and maturation. The recurrent journey in these works, in the familiar territory of Mineo as well as in fantastic, allegorical regions, moves toward the discovery of an ultimate immortality or integration in the universal life of the cosmos; although the quest often appears to remain fruitless, when it is not clearly a failure.

After *Dolcissimo,* Bonaviri dedicated several years to poetry, publishing *Il dire celeste* and *O corpo sospiroso,* and to short stories in *Novelle saracene*; he edited the verse and stories of his youth in *Nel silenzio della luna, Di fumo cilestrino,* and *Quark*; and his literary criticism in *L'arenario* before turning again to the novel in *È un rosseggiar di peschi e d'albicocchi* and *Il dormiveglia* (1988). His work has been widely translated, into French and Spanish, as well as German, Swedish, Polish, Czech, Russian, and Chinese.

Dolcissimo seems to me an ideal work with which to introduce Bonaviri to the English-reading public, because it is deeply characteristic of the author's work as a whole. As with many of his novels, the structure is that of a journey, a quest, or a series of quests, which move toward the ultimate journey into death and a region beyond time. Rather than the text of an official inquiry, as the opening paragraph suggests, it is the story of a journey in search of the material for an inquiry, at the end of which the text of the inquiry will not be written because the inquirers will have embraced the destiny of the most deeply questioning of the Zebulonians and disappeared into the subterranean world where he has preceded them in search of new dimensions of life.

For the narrator, Ariete, the journey is also a return to his birthplace, to his mother's house, after years of absence. But his visit finds the town prey to a relentless process of disintegration, due primarily to emigration and the consequent neglect to which fields and buildings are subject. The destructive action of the weather, since cultivation and repair have ceased, has become dramatic; even the meager rainfall and the harsh vegetation it produces concur with the drought and the incessant winds to scarify the landscape and lay bare curious natural phenomena, which become the obsessive object of the narrator's descriptions. And the absence of so many of the townspeople, together with the deterioration due to their emigration, produce negative influences on the remaining population of women, children, and the old, social and psychological developments on which Ariete's friend and interlocutor, the "ethnopsychiatrist" Mario Sinus, speculates freely.

The journey, however, does not end with these discoveries and their highly imaginative representation in the novel; it also leads to a rich evocation of the Zebulonia of the past, on at least two levels of temporal distance: to the rediscovery of the geological, archaeological, and historical past of Zebulonia, and to the nostalgic reevocation of the Zebulonia of the narrator's childhood and adolescence, the kind of journey Bonaviri has called "mnemonautics," the journey into the dimension of "ancestral memory."

If the imagination of the writer endows a parched landscape in a dire state of abandonment and inexorable deterioration with menacing wonder, the past nostalgically evoked by Ariete, by contrast, turns the Zebulonia of his childhood into an earthly paradise – not a lush tropical paradise but a semiarid, middle-eastern land of Eden, rich in spices and perfumes, aromatic herbs, exotic and exquisite fruits, rare birds, an Eden made richer still by the arts of its inhabitants, the sauces and marzipans of Ariete's mother, his grandfather's breads, the sweets made by the sisters in the seven convents, the embroidery of the Zebulonian women, the poetry, the music, the craftsmanship of the artisans of Zebulonia.

The central figure in this Eden is Dolcissimo, whose very name suggests a concentration of its sweetness, and whose presence in the remembered time of the work contrasts with his virtual absence in its present time. A simple man who lives in poverty, Dolcissimo is also a mediator between nature and human beings, presiding as the mysterious genius of the place over all the arts, the customs, and significant events of the Zebulonia of the dimension of memory, and especially over the deepening of the sensory, mental, and spiritual perceptions of his townspeople. As his mortal adventure approaches its end, Dolcissimo is found in the caverns beneath the cemetery undergoing a mysterious metamorphosis, and is recognized by the people of Zebulonia as their god, the embodiment, within extreme material poverty, of spiritual humility, absence of greed, and the creative impulse, the deeply human qualities that in all religions of the humble are a source of wisdom and consolation.

To an even greater degree than other of Bonaviri's works, *Dolcissimo* incorporates autobiographical elements – the attachments of the author's youth (his parents, the aunt and uncle he lived with, the places and pleasures of his childhood), his later aspirations (his frustrated dream of a career as a research scientist), his adult frustrations as a Public Health officer, the profound nostalgia of his later years and its translation into mythic imagery. Thus not only Ariete, the doctor returning to his native Mineo-Zebulonia, but the outsiders Sinus and Melange, and all the Zebulonians as well, express aspects of Bonaviri's experience, all share the poetry of his animistic-scientific vision of reality, and all, therefore, speak basically the same language. And because the vision is a poetic vision, the language is a poetic language.

Bonaviri's is neither the primitive religious-animistic vision of his ancestors, nor the scientific world-view of the modern physician. His is "an altogether different poetic intuition," as he once called it, a synthesis of the animism and pantheism inherited from his ancestral culture and the post-Einsteinian cosmology of his formal education, "different in the sense that its breadth is greater, that it attempts to reflect the deeply disturbing way we live now."[1] And it fuses the language of the two cultures in a poetry itself surely "different" from any other, a unique voice.

From the very first pages of the novel, the reader experiences this fusion, because the movement of each section – often of individual paragraphs,

1. Biographical data and Bonaviri's statements on his beliefs and his poetics can be found in Giuseppe Bonaviri, "Autobiografia di uno scrittore," *Archivio Storico per la Sicilia Orientale*, 76, 1 (1980):313-22 (from which all the quotations in this introduction are drawn); idem, *La follia* (Catania: Società di Storia Patria per la Sicilia Orientale, 1976), pp. 19-39; and in Rodolfo Di Biasio, *Giuseppe Bonaviri* (Firenze: La Nuova Italia, 1978), pp. 3-8; and Franco Zangrilli, "Incontro con Giuseppe Bonaviri," *La Fusta*, 6, 1-2 (Spring-Fall 1981):3-41.

sometimes indeed of single sentences – parallels that of the entire novel, which begins with the official assignment of a scientific inquiry to two doctors, and ends with their immersion in a mysterious dimension of life outside time. The first section begins on an apparently realistic note, rational, faintly bureaucratic:

> The Department of Public Health has invited me, in my capacity as physician...to conduct an investigation....

And moves through an accumulation of what appears to be meticulous scholarly detail[2] – geological, historical, botanical – into which strange elements gradually intrude, toward the frankly fantastic, even the surreal: in the Capuchin monastery of Zebulonia a human-cypress hybrid stands, with

> eyes of tremulous matter expressing salty fear, a shortened body, and a leafy darkness at temples, hands and shins.

Dolcissimo often abandons ordinary logic, in fact, and makes the startling, dreamlike leaps we associate with modern poetry. Meaning may be carried in some passages more by sound, rhythm, sequences of objective correlatives, an almost hypnotic pleasure and trust in the resources of language itself. Bonaviri's prose disconcerts our rational expectations again and again, creating its own logic as poetry does. The long poem of Part V, with its unexpected, sometimes cryptic images and

---

2. The key to many of these details may be found in the author's and translator's notes, which appear at the end of the book in a separate section.

Introduction

its idiosyncratic diction, differs from the prose in which it is embedded less in kind than in compression. This translation attempts to convey the complexity and flexibility of Bonaviri's style, to be faithful to its frequent deviations from the familiar patterns of standard Italian prose, to approximate its many idiosyncrasies and the extraordinary liberties which it often takes with the language.

In its synthesis of the animistic and the scientific, of the ancestral and the modern, Bonaviri's language expresses the pain of the contemporary individual caught in a violent crisis of passage, the anguish and restlessness of an age of rapid and destabilizing change. Historically bound to our anthropocentric view, comforted for centuries by faith in a transcendental immortality, we find ourselves facing the possibility that our immortal spirits, experienced primarily in the reality of thought, may be nothing more than the product of chemical processes occurring in the brain, a phenomenon altogether ephemeral and mortal. However, in Bonaviri's view the "restless children of our time" still long to "emerge from their deepening mortal solitude" through "channels of time still undefined, unfamiliar, and certainly alien to our ordinary notion of time-space," still long "to return in a self-renewing vital cycle," to live by a different notion of time. This process of salvation is the new task of poetry, of the "mythmaking utopia" that in our time "has become a means of self-liberation." It implies a necessary process of "deconstruction of humanity's historical notion of itself;" the "most compelling" modern psychological and phenomenological theories point to "numerous possibilities of creating time and space around us" in "a reality expanding to become anthropocosmic."

Thus the first principle in Bonaviri's thinking is the recognition of the "triadic relationship of human beings-plants-stone," the community of all elements of the cosmos, which undergo continuous evolution and transformation; it embraces the possibility – and perhaps the reality – that "thinking matter" moves throughout the entire cosmos, that all parts of the cosmos are able to think – "an immense thinking sea," a "noosphere," including people, animals, trees, stones – "though with different degrees of awareness;" and that this movement occurs along "time lines" in "streams of free atoms" or "psychic remnants," in "elementary thinking particles," or simply as "pulsing." All of which is for Bonaviri a kind of recasting in poetic terms of quantum thinking. The critical moments for that movement are the moments of passage, "in anthropocosmic terms, from the shores of life to the complex shores of death," an obsessively recurring motif in Bonaviri, which "among other things, can be seen as the irruption of anguish into our everyday life." At the critical moment of "biological death," the "psychic entities in which, in quantum language, the activity of thought develops and is organized in us," are scattered "in atomic currents of dispersion," but later "the dispersed elementary particles of our spirit" tend to concentrate again as in "a black hole, to use a recent cosmological reference." In Bonaviri's thought "there exists a shadowy area of 'possibles' in which the spatialization of such thinking particles might be infinite." And if so, in the caverns where the Zebulonian dead are gathered or in the darkness of intergalactic space where *Martedina*'s astronauts end up, death transforms the individual into an "elemental flow of thinking atoms," into a "post-mortal pulsing;" what remains is substantially memory, a memory that is fundamentally nostalgic, a desire "to walk anew along inverted time lines reaching up toward the sunlit region of an earth green with affections and trees." And for the living, death in these terms is "a search for the shores of light, liberating them from existential anguish" – a "metamorphosis, in sum, that becomes, even in its fertile desperation, a liberating 'religion.'"

In Bonaviri's work our complex apprehension of reality in the modern world and the intricate web of our restless anguish are reflected in the complexity of the language in which the author expresses both that vision and that anguish. Thus the voices of his novels and poems are engaged in a kind of translation "of our language, which today has so many levels, so many sources," into an original idiom. The style of Bonaviri's artistic maturity fuses a multiplicity of linguistic resources, including what the author has called the "alchemic-fantastic" and the "archaic-dialectal," with "lexical derivations from biology, physics, psychoanalysis, relativity and quantum theories, et cetera." Breaking with the restraints of ordinary logic, his language is "an upheaval, a ferment of multiple meanings, refractions of original motifs, where there exists only one true 'topic' – imagined, dreamed, remembered – the ubiquity of our restless spirit."

A style so unique, so inventive, will clearly resist translation, particularly in a language as different from Italian as English. To render *Dolcissimo* in English has been a labor of patient love. My wife, Alice Gladstone Mariani, whose creative mastery of her native English has always been of invaluable help to me, worked closely with me on the final version of this text. The credit is hers, if this translation has achieved some measure of its objectives: precision, idiomatic ease, fluidity, and an approximation of the poetry of the original.

Umberto Mariani

I

The Department of Public Health has invited me in my capacity as physician, along with my friend, Mario Sinus, to conduct an investigation into the beliefs, attitudes, and plain blind errors to which my home town has fallen prey.

Called Menàinon by the Hellenes, meaning a lofty, solitary place, Qalàt Minàw by the Arabs for a lonely, wild hill, and today Zebulonia,* my town is located on a mountain 37.15 degrees north and 14.44° east of Greenwich. Legend has it that it was founded in the fifth century B.C. by Ducetius, the king of the Siculi,† who, until taken prisoner, fought the Greek colonizers from the coastal regions. To the capes, basins, hollows, and steep declivities that bound my island the tides in the past, rushing by the legs of the fishermen, brought live fish rich in chloride, iodine, and sulphur absorbed from plankton. Now those shores have become gorges and twisting valleys where an occasional old woman fishes from the bluish sediments gilt-heads, herrings, and sardines, already dead.

In times immemorial, in addition to their pictographic numbers and purple cloth, the Phoenicians had brought the art of minting to Zebulonia. Until the time of Agathocles, during the 115th Olympiad, when L. Plautius and Marius Fulvus were consuls in Rome, no human image was ever imprinted on coins, as Diodorus Siculus‡ informs us. Instead, the cities depicted on them the

1

emblems of their particular cults: the stalk of grain rising from the furrow, the vessel in which meals were prepared, the eagle pointing to the lightning bolt issuing from the zodiac.

The subsoil of Zebulonia is made up of sedimentary rocks, the age of which stretches back from five million to a hundred million years into the Messinian era. During the last century it has been shaken by at least a thousand earthquakes, one thousand twenty-seven, to be precise, according to the records of the seismic monitoring station directed by Corrado Guzzanti since 1940. These substrata have an overlapping drift in a north-west and west-south-east direction, thus creating an epicenter of rocky folds that lead horizontally toward Kalàt-Yeròn, Plaza Hermosa, Ganz, and, in the opposite direction, toward concentric Ochiolà, Millestelle, wheat-rich Burchiaturo, and Kalè Eubèa. According to the geologists, the orogen lies six thousand meters deep, under localities once inhabited by farmers, hunters, gleaners, almond pickers, lemon peddlers, stone gatherers.* The faults join the mountain on your right as you climb up to the town. One must mention the high magnitude earthquake that on January 11, 1693 razed Zebulonia to the ground together with the remains of the burial niches of the necropolis of Trinacia, a Sicilian town rising on the Timucah plateau.† Owing to that tremendous seism, in the region of Zebulonia, out of the loamy navels of Mt. Catalfaro, where Erice once stood, came sharp-edged stones, siliceous swords, golden pebbles, while in the low fertile plain, where Ducetius had built Palíca, Lake Naftía, once used for pagan rites, vomited black liquid, masks of royal

2

mummies, and wooden heads of women crowned with turquoise and lapis lazuli.

Because at that time the chroniclers were mostly churchmen, they recorded the earthquakes (on a map that carried a small trumpet-playing god as a coat of arms) in terms of the damages inflicted on churches, monasteries, and castles. Regarding the aforementioned seismic event, in the register of the parish of St. Peter's, among shadows cast by an enormous crucifix, was written in church Latin: "Year of our Lord 1693. January 11th. On this day, by an earthquake that was visited upon us, the whole town together with all its churches was destroyed, and two thousand people died whose names were not recorded, who were buried without rites or funerals; while other people died as a consequence of the same event weeks later."[*]

Ibn Zafèr, author of, among other things, *Solwan el motà*,[†] that is, *Political Consolations* (of which a valuable edition was published by Le Monnier in 1851, edited by Amari), in his book, *Historical Notes on Zebulonia*,[‡] printed in Noto by Zammit, wrote regarding that earthquake: "The royal military commander Giantommaso de Guerriero, after a life of turpitude, turned to the Catholic religion following the premature loss of his young daughter, the former princess of Biscaro. So in 1588 he constructed the large building that became the residence of Jesuits from every corner of the island. The edifice having been destroyed by the dreadful earthquake of 1693, the followers of Jesus rebuilt it using the two thousand seven hundred peasants who had survived, whom they divided into two groups. One was given the task of salvaging the pediments, pillars, arches, and blocks of stone

of the Norman castle of Zebulonia, turned to rubble
by the seism; the other was made to carry water in
jugs, ewers, and buckets, from creeks flowing in the
nearby valleys. Those who did not own beasts of
burden stood side by side in endless lines, passing
the containers along. Those poor Zebulonians ate
edible weeds, fava beans, and bran mush. The
twelve ruined towers of the castle were used by the
Jesuits to build a large terrace on which an unusual
hanging garden was created. Many exotic plants
were imported by merchant sailors trafficking with
the land of the rising sun – black spice trees,
coconut palms, the first persimmons, loquats,
crimson flowers that swell toward morning,
pomegranates, Phrygian figs of the very sweet
brogiotto kind, sensitive plants whose leaves
withdraw before the summer heat."

From the same Ibn Zafèr we learn that the gates
of the castle were used by the Jesuits to rebuild the
four entrances to Zebulonia: the Odigítria, the
Udientiam, the Iacò, also called the gate of
Bacchus, and the one named after the hero
Adinolfo.* With the stones of the destroyed
houses, the Capuchin friars made the necessary
repairs to their monastery, which still rises on the
little hill where the cemetery was built around
1850. These monks took advantage of the religious
sentiments of the women, who, helped by their
children, willingly hauled sand, pyrites, ochres,
muds, roots, pitted stones, agates, opals, and virgin
soils in baskets and chests. Thus, in less than ten
years the town once again had, in greater numbers
than before, its churches and temples, its places
suited to meditation. The Jesuits began once again
to teach their patrician students, who came from all

4

over to learn patristics, liturgy, techniques of making sterile trees fertile, the Old and the New Testament according to Jesuit doctrines. They also set up all sorts of clocks in Zebulonia, giving preference to the solar ones easy to paint on street corners and the facades of churches, to make the peasants aware of the relentless flow of time. Without the Jesuits' intervention, on the other hand, thanks to pollination by tender winds, rickety little plants originating from the hanging garden sprang up on the roofs of the town from the dust blown in from the fields. The strangest graft made by the Jesuits was that of the tuttifrutti tree. They succeeded in obtaining a tree that, both on its main crown and on the shoots that thrust themselves into the ground and shot up again farther and farther in endless growth, produced different fruits on each branch: the apricot, the quince, the bitter orange, the crystalline grape, azaroles, jujubes, sorb-apples, pears, persimmons, prickly pears. The real grafting miracle was the lul-daghelí, mentioned by Della Valle in his seventeenth-century *Travels,* which could be considered a successful cross of about twenty types of fruit. Oval near the stem, it became hexagonal, then bumpy, then suddenly scaly with smooth protrusions; it was of a rosy color and as sleek as velvet in some places. Since it contained small amounts of coral powders, its flavor seems to have been at once like honey and orange blossom shading into civet, bitter-sweet, figlike, with, perhaps, a touch of cinnamon. From both the tree and the fruit those priests derived fragrant juleps, digestive teas, and the so-called angelwater, highly aromatic, smelling of rushes, citron oil, musk, and amber. With angelwater they

5

perfumed the delicate fans with mother-of-pearl
handles with which they kept themselves cool in the
canicular hours, strolling in that garden from which
one could see all of Zebulonia. There they composed doctrinal epistles, parallel biographies of
saints, rational explanations of dogma, subtle
lustral poems. As evening drew near, the peasants
gathered in the square below to enjoy the lightest
breath of that perfume called by the women
"precious tear of the Lord."

Ibn Zafèr also informs us that the Capuchin
fathers, accustomed to afternoon repose, lulled by
the villagers' singsong chants to their donkeys
turning round and round in the sunny threshing
yards, eventually rebuilt their library. Together
with the incunabula, the most prominent works
were those of the missionary Ludovico Buglio, a
Zebulonian who died in China in 1682 with the
title of mandarin, having translated into the
language of that country the *Summa theologica* of
Thomas Aquinas. In addition these monks had
become accustomed, generation after generation, to
sheltering Byzantine heretics, Spanish warriors,
fugitive Arabs who, undertaking the study of
alchemy and of the exact sciences, ended up by
writing unorthodox commentaries on the Koran.
One of these was Ibn Zafèr, who left the monastery
books like *El Tafsir cabir,* that is, *The Great
Commentary* on the Koran, and *El Giannah fi I'tikad
ahl es sunnah,* which means, *Paradise in the Sunnite
Faith.* But the Capuchins had a real predilection for
the construction of telescopes, with which, in the
depth of the most harrowing darkness, they
explored the fires and minerals falling from the sky.
Friar Onorio, whom we will meet as a very old man

in this story, followed the course of the comet of von Biela, which had also been seen by Secchi in August of 1852. It appears from his book *On the Moving and Finite Universe* that, by studying meteoric particles and the gentle movements of the heliotropes that filled the small cells of the monastery and determining through the spectrum the very high temperatures of the interstellar clouds, he arrived at the conclusion that the stars had moved into the orbicular universe through continual expansion. His observation that some trees have a very long life also sparked an interest in biology. Of course, he was thinking in particular of the cypress, that can live up to five thousand years; the nearby cemetery was full of such trees, which, exuding incense, softened one's transmigrating thoughts.

He made potions from the bark, the leaves, and the red racemes, but soon realized that the ingestion of such mixtures only strengthened the limbs and the wonders of the imagination. Ibn Zafèr at page 87 informs us that to cast off evil thoughts that came to him after hearing the confessions of cheats and swindlers, he would have liked, had the technical knowledge of the age allowed him, to send the elect among the dead into the astral orbits of Venus, Mars, and Jupiter; but being unable to do so, he judged that to achieve an extension of their lives he had to do something very different. According to Zafèr (although we are still dubious about this) he joined the essence of the cypress seed to the female ovum, which through successively increasing cellular circles developed into a horrifying being; this he joined, by grafting arteries, veins, and lymph ducts, to a cypress that

7

rose in the monastery's atrium, in order to give it the longest possible life. The result must have been a being with a coarse green face, eyes of tremulous matter expressing salty fear, a shortened body, and a leafy darkness at temples, hands, and shins. Many times a day, as he looked at it, Friar Onorio would run to read the following verses of repentance from a sura of the Koran: "Allâh, my brothers, will take the indignation from your hearts and will turn benevolently to those who believe. Allâh is sage and full of wisdom."

II

"This way they go who would go into peace,"* the ethnopsychiatrist Mario Sinus quoted, smiling, as we advanced on foot (our car having broken down) through broom and thyme. Around us, from height to height, rugged spurs closed ranks in the direction of Zebulonia, over which the luminous sunset flared, splendid against dark spaces.

The investigation had been entrusted to us by one Ida Melange, any of whose features of appearance or character were hard to imagine. She was known to us through a little treatise, *De amore mutatis mutandis*,† in which, with an eye to keeping vice and corruption at bay, she discusses the incorporeal things that reflect the soul of the world.

Far ahead of us a falcon, winging the hot updraft, grew smaller and smaller, way up there, to our narrowed eyes. Far away, below, beyond the dusty green of the orange groves, among pockets of vapor, rose the exploratory rigs of the Exxon Company. Except for those dying groves, you saw only bare fields, which up until thirty years ago produced from ten to fifteen million kilos of wheat and fava beans, measured in *tumoli*. These were cylindrical containers, made of carob or walnut wood, followed in decreasing order by similar smaller containers, the *mondello* and the *carozzo*. The local noble families studded the borders of

9

these cylinders with polished silver and precious stones. They were measures of Norman origin.

Grains were cultivated at that time at Violo, Ruccuvè, Sparagogna, on the banks of Ferro Creek, at Cameni, among the rocks of the Coste, on the estate of Castelluccio, around Lake Naftía, and, if you raised your eyes as I was asking Mario Sinus to do, you could see fava beans, barley, wheat at the Pietre Nere, on the slopes of Mount Catalfaro, in the valley of Donna Ragusa, and also, in the same direction, at Albano Bianco, at Malati, and proceeding downward, at Nicchiara as well, and further up, on the Càllari Plateau, or, coming back, among the crags of the Trezzito, at Camúti, Gianforte, at Vattàno, at Fiumecaldo, along ravines and ditches, and in so many localities that my friend asked, "How many localities around Zebulonia have names?"

The fields of Indian corn, spelt, hard wheat and soft, mingled in waves of yellow with the blooming mustard and the fava beans that condensed the rising dew, gathering the obliging moonlight under their leaves.

"This must have been a sea," exclaimed Mario Sinus. "Eating the tiny seeds of mustard," he added, "helps one to meditate on the physical world."

We continued to climb the mountain rapidly, while my friend said, "In a field of wheat one's hearing grows sharper, Ariete, and one's voice, like a vibrating body, becomes visible as it harmoniously bends the ear of grain." He added that the wheat kernel, with its floury substance and milky fluid, makes for a restorative bread that mellows the senses. In Zebulonia, in fact, in spite of the semiarid climate due to the scarcity of rainfall, between the pebbles and the fossil-rich sand there is a humusy soil that forms an aggregate with ferrous concretions when storms swell the creeks; their alluvial waters carry clays and auriferous nuggets downstream, causing the bedrock of the sea floor to emerge.

Because of its rather stony soil, Zebulonia did not have many groves. Nevertheless, it produced walnuts, almonds, apricots, blackberries and mulberries, cherries, figs, and in the fall capers, peaches, apples, medlars, onions, garlic, mushrooms. Some people even owned the tuttifrutti tree we have mentioned, or cultivated red peppers in open patches and, if they watched out carefully for the early frost, the reddish bunches of seven-flavor grapes. Food was obtained from roots, saplings, leaves, dandelions, chicories. The smells, colors, and sounds of these fruits were carried to the brain by the thin blood.

All this time I was urging Mario Sinus to look back at the great arc of the eastern mountains.

"Ariete," he said, "in the appendix to the *De amore mutatis mutandis* Ida Melange has studied the relationship between plowed fields and the winds. According to her, the north wind, by freezing the vapors of caves, sweeps away the rotten effluvia of the fields. The east wind makes the rising sun look asymmetrical, dissolving its rays into motes. The tumultuous west wind greatly enhances the aromas of thyme, catmint, and oregano."

"It may be true," I answered. "The air of Zebulonia, in fact, used to be good for sores, head wounds, and the weak constitution of the old.

11

According to common belief, garlic, onions, and olive oil were good for worms. Lettuce and wild fennel increased the flow of milk in women. Canicular fevers were alleviated with infusions of wormwood and holy-thistle."

The great mountainside we were climbing was covered with wormwood and thistle. You could see their white corymbs and red flower-heads around dead tree trunks, on the flinty patches where we were already beginning to encounter boys and old men. As I climbed I began to realize that as a consequence of massive emigration the land had been radically changed: there were no more olive trees, no agave, no birds to drink the rain.

"Come on," Sinus tried to console me, "think of the new things we're going to encounter. You'll see, we'll do a good piece of research. You can be sure of it."

I did not answer. The earth had taken on a different physical shape, extruding clays, roots, geodes, schists.

"Listen," Sinus observed, "the different aspect of the countryside creates different feelings in those of your countrymen that have remained."

We saw kidney-shaped burls of dried-up wild olives full of dead earthworms. The surface of the soil exhibited purplish ferrous deposits and peculiar, indefinable nodules.

"The sun's refraction," the psychiatrist went on, "is different in these places."

In my opinion the greatest damage occurs in October and March, pivotal months, so to speak, since in October the light has diminished so much that the saline spirits of the fields, in which our eyes are mirrored, increase; in March, as in April, the humors melt at the foot of the almond trees and in the soil and correspondingly mortal flesh is weaker.

The rainfall did not exceed four hundred millimeters a year and was quickly dried up by the north wind that had destroyed the carob trees of the slopes, leaving them mere wood flattened to the ground. The filtering water and the telluric gases themselves had allowed the inferior terrestrial forces to gain the upper hand. Because light and the eye are one, after all, the fields looked as if they were strewn with decaying snakes and spiders.

"What a strange wasteland!" sighed Mario Sinus. And pointing to some protrusions in a crevice he added, "Let's look at them. They have a strange gleam."

They were branched scales, malleable and soft enough to scratch with a fingernail. "It is copper," Sinus said.

The free crystals, of a shiny rose color, were very few: most of the copper was threadlike, brown with oxidation, with some intrusions of azurite. On certain mushroom-shaped stones there were imprints of pecten, of the kind that surfaced as scallop shells at Timucah on the gray mound that we, brother Timor, used to cross to reach the well. We used to play on it, right there on what had been an ocean bed, and was now rock resounding to hail and thunder.

A few boys were collecting moon stones in the gullies.

"What do you do with them?" Sinus asked. Not knowing us, they made off, asking over their shoulders: "What's it to you?"

We approached an old man, greeted him. I used the Zebulonian dialect to gain his good will since he eyed us with suspicion. He was putting some crates of copper ore on a donkey's back. "What are they for?" I asked.

He said, "What are you looking for? Don't you know this land has been abandoned by God?"

"Do you come to collect them often?"

"Do you think I eat stones?"

Other old men were digging here and there with hoes and shovels, and a few with picks walked up to us. They wore caps against the July heat.

Sinus asked himself whether these rural folk had not already fallen under the influence of the stony element that certainly was triggering other reactive mechanisms in them. Meanwhile the children we had disturbed were shouting, "Why don't you leave? What do you want from us?"

Under the peasants' guidance, the young Zebulonians were extracting things from prisms of earth, from clods overrun by crabgrass – bones, sword pommels, chipped gray vases, cracked black flasks. Due to the unusual angle of refraction, the sunlight on those objects constantly changed color.

We also noticed a clay lacrimal vase that an old man had pulled out of a crevice. Seeing that we were watching him, he told us that among the Zebulonians there still existed the fountain of tears that dispelled the black humors from the heart. Further up, a pale boy had found an encrusted ring in a culvert, while another had pulled a fibula, a bowl, and a spiral ornament from a cave.

"I am giving them to you," he smiled. He handed them to us and ran uphill. A few old men, grown more trusting, showed us some coins, taking them from baskets where they lay among chips of copper. They cleaned them with their large red handkerchiefs, and showed them to us; one even said, "Take them. They're yours." On one you could make out the Greek inscription *Mena, inon;* some bore a laurel-crowned head of Apollo and on the back the face of Asclepius; two bore the bearded image of Heracles holding his club. They were poor relics worn by time, thin and chipped. Two coins were given us on impulse by the pale boy ("Here, take them," he said); one depicted Demeter, crowned with ears of wheat, the himation on her head; the other, with the words, *Menai, non,* bore the imprint of the figure of Hermes holding the caduceus. Sinus took great interest in these finds; he even gave money to those who gave him coins, some of which were offered with roots of myrtle and wild fennel still attached to them. As the news got around that we were paying, other children came down the slope. Some of them might have been five years old.

"Hey, you," they shouted, "buy from me! me!"

I explained to Sinus that the coins bearing the word *Mena,* even if the imprint were worn away, went back to the Greek mintage in Zebulonia. But the strata that yielded those pieces were not the same; they appeared to belong to different ages. We succeeded in collecting ten coins in all. On one, rusted around the rim, we saw an owl with round, hypnotizing eyes. Another must have been Judaic, for it bore the image of Simon Maccabee, and one last numismatic fossil, attributable to Guglielmo il Malo, William the Bad, displayed on the obverse a palm grove with five trees.

"Ariete," Sinus said, "if you clink them, they don't all sound the same. This one, for instance, rings sumptuously, reminding me of the present month of July; this other one from ancient Mena, or Zebulonia, which lay amidst the azurite, has a soft sound that reminds one of the delicate herb dittany, and of one's mother's voice."

"I hear it, Sinus, I hear it," I told him.

Clinking now one fossil, now the other, he went on: "Whether silver or bronze, or even only stone, money has not always signified damnation and vanity, because it carries within it the infinite desires of men, and the previous life of the electrons bound in their metals. Which, as we know, have a splendid luster, turn diaphanous in the light of dawn, and in the fall retain a tempered heat. I believe, Ariete, that in these places, the gravitation of the earth is more intense. Do you know what Ida Melange says somewhere in her essay? Listen: 'Enter a small cave in July and sit where the earth is warmer to hear her pulsations. They are tiny magnetic events, spiral-shaped, open at one end: there, capture the particles called gravitons, and you will step into non-time.'"

As evening could now be seen in the valley, the old men called the children together: "Let's go, it's getting late."

They came out of fissures in the ground, from stony slopes, from shade-dappled embankments, from the stubble, and most of them followed the peasants who were going up the mountain with sacks on their shoulders, or crates neatly strapped on the donkeys. But some of the boys said: "Why do we have to come with you? Are you hens that we've got to follow you like chicks? We're going towards the Pietre Nere where we can find other things to amuse us while it's still light, and we'll pray at the boulder the god of the poor sleeps under."

16

Seen from above, the mountainside seemed tormented by hundreds of holes, by mounds and limestone trenches.

"Thank you," we said. "We'll see you again."

And we started off again, walking quickly among the low caper bushes. As we reached the first houses of Zebulonia, Mario Sinus exclaimed, "What silence!"

In the Varanna quarter a woman pulled a goat along, a peasant went homeward with a load of branches, hens fluttered about in the dust. The poor dwellings attracted Sinus' interest: the walls were cracked, the wood of the front doors was split, strips of dark cloth had been nailed to them as a sign of mourning.

"How many new facts for our inquiry," observed Mario Sinus. "It seems to me that each thing gives off its own space, so to speak. Each is surrounded by a kind of unique projection of forces, which we should calculate correctly for our inquiry."

The wind had risen, coming in waves from the few Saracen olive trees down valley and the blazing boulders on the slopes. As we climbed, my friend gazed at the roofs on which the last splendor of evening was dying. The underlayer of woven reeds could be seen sticking out here and there from under the rooftiles. The chimneys looked yellow amid the drifting sunlit motes. All this gave an immense feeling of space that exerted a powerful attraction on the eye and on the sulphureous movement of the light itself. The animal spirit of the wind had thickened on the balconies and on the olive green thresholds. Some women were hanging out hempen cloths, dyed with sumac, and saffron-dyed linen.

17

"Why do they do that?" my friend asked.

"My guess would be, to disperse the wind."

In fact, due to the turbulence of the sunlight at that hour, the wind had gotten stronger, but its gusts were broken into a thousand strands by the hanging drapery.

The buildings were of the kind that had always been there, a mixture of Arabic and Norman with a touch of Andalusia and Catalonia. For mortar, sand and lime were used both outside and inside, where the only vents were the rather small windows. The foundations lay on intrusive rock of pebbly aggregate. Most of the houses had only one story, some two, made of stones brought down from mountaintops. The wood used was olive, or oak, or carob, trees, that is, which disperse humidity and mildly filter the sunlight. Exceptionally cornel wood, or the cold willow was used. Larch, ash, and the trees of the valley floor were practically unknown. Many of the dwellings leaned slightly, due to past microseisms, but according to Sinus it was a case of deliberate self-orientation in a southerly direction so they could enjoy up to their very chimneys the perfumed flora that the mild spring temperature brought out on the eroded slopes.

"Ariete," the psychiatrist said, "we must take into consideration the probable sensory perceptions of these poor dwellings, since they are one with their inhabitants."

In the past the rooftops truly represented a physical extension of the Zebulonians even when the moon rose over them, enormous on the heels of the night. Unfortunately now there were old bones up there, skins of dead cats, and soil that permitted the growth of parietaria, puffballs, and saplings in colors from purple to indigo, originating from the lost hanging garden of the Jesuits. They were dwarf wild figtrees, pomegranates and quinces one foot high, pricklypear cactuses on which the wind left long white hair. The balconies, the dormers, the galleries were full of old women. Some were combing their hair slowly with primitive hardwood combs. They collected the hair that either came loose or was cut on purpose, in small baskets: matted gray tufts and little white tails that stirred in the wind as if through some sensitive animation of their own. In the distance the voice of the man who came from Càtana to buy it ("O you women, I buy hair!") could be heard. Those locks or balls of hair would be swapped for dishes, forks, aprons, knives. They would be used in wigs, ceremonial braid, pillows, even headbands for statues. Most of those old women were picking fruits from the plants rooted in the fissures in the walls: the tiniest figs, hazel-nuts, and the sweetest little grapes, whose juices some were pressing into mugs.

They signalled our unexpected arrival to each other with gestures and sighs. Some shut themselves indoors in order not to be looked at, others climbed out to the roofs through the dormers and continued to collect sticks, diaphanous peaches, and nests built by the sparrows among those tiny trees.

"Who could have imagined a spectacle like this?" Sinus said to me.

"As you can see," I answered sadly, "emigration has not meant wealth for Zebulonia."

Because of the steepness of the slope, the houses leaned on each other and we noticed that the pots of rue and basil on the windowsills were held in

19

place by thin copper bands, which in other places, cleverly interlaced, braced up primitive lintels, steps, and slanting walls.

"Ariete," my friend observed, "from the lumps of copper that the old men gathered in baskets they make things up here to shore up what is coming loose. I understand why on the tourist maps your town is called *Zebulonia-of-bronze*. They want to attract tourists."

Along the outside walls of sheepfolds we saw spiral ammonites mixed in with leafy fossils. Embedded in the walls of an abandoned house we were able to distinguish two coins of Greek origin, from which the image of an owl gazed at us. My psychologist friend told me in an undertone that in such a rural community on its way to extinction an arcane wisdom was innate.

"Ariete," he concluded, "as you know, copper gleams, attracts fine vapors and, regulating the universality of things with its brilliant eye, gives rise to unusual ideas."

In corners, under the eaves, in the backyards, coins and bronzes chimed, perhaps because the wind racing down the roofs was amplified by the foliage of the little trees.

"Oh, Ariete!" I heard somebody call. "How come you are here? Don't you know the town's been taken over by owls?"

It was a woman, over eighty, with white hair and a very wrinkled face.

"Why did you come back?" she went on. "Don't you remember me?"

Oh, of course, it was Yaluna, who lived just below our house, in a lean-to, from the rafters of which she hung oranges still attached to their branches, little bundles of oregano, tomatoes, azaroles.

"Oh, Yaluna," I exclaimed. We embraced.

In our town, my brother Timor, the old women, due to their past sorrows and their longing for their children, are deeply wrinkled on the forehead and around the eyes, the points where the mind's energy concentrates.

"Ariete, my son," Yaluna wailed, "my husband, Massaro Giuseppe,* is dead, and my son doesn't come back from Switzerland any more. You grew up among us and when you became a doctor and could help us, you went away."

"Oh, don't fret about that now, please. Come, tell me," I asked the woman, to distract her from the grief with which she looked at me, "what happened to the shoemakers who lived in this neighborhood?"

"There were many of them here in the Varanna quarter. Now, some have changed trades, some have gone to Argentina, some have died. The last of them was Turi Vilardo; he wasn't yet seventy when Salamanca the barber found him dead among his awls and hammers. His hands were already blue, and an eye-socket half empty. An owl was asleep on his neck."

She pointed to the hovels built against a wall: some were wood, others stone, three were nothing more than tiny caves.

"They lived there, Ariete, remember? Only a few had their shops in other neighborhoods, like Don Mimí Manusía, who taught shoemaking to your Uncle Antonio. But now, as I told you, the town's been taken over by the owls. But where are you going? Would you like me to go with you?"

She was carrying a basket in which she had gathered some mallow and chicory. In silence she walked with us toward the quarter called Santa Maria, listening to Mario Sinus who was observing in a low voice that the owl, classified as *asio otus,* is usually found in rocky areas. His penchant for hooting becomes especially intense in July (and it was July 11, my birthday) because, the leafy parts of the cinnamon and spice trees having dried up, the effusion of their aromas is at its peak, and even sharper in the direction of Orion already visible in the stellar arc. We were walking slowly so that the woman could keep up with us. In the western sky the sun had been engulfed in darkness.

"Zebulonia," the psychiatrist was explaining, "is experiencing disintegration. We must find out what obsessions feed the spirit of the old and the young who are left."

In his opinion, if we were to find a parallel obsession in both of them, we would have to surmise that they were no longer capable of assimilating motion and therefore time; if the obsessions were not parallel, then it would mean that each individual organized a space for himself out of his own experience, and remained isolated in his notion of place and time.

I felt somewhat dejected, fearing that we could never complete such a complicated inquiry. Since the sunset was over, and there was not a streak of sunlight left, nor a last angry ray, the women were coming out on the balconies in the streets below the castle. Some were wearing the customary black kerchief on their heads; most of them were all decked out with shawls and rings. Down below, with aromatic fumes a few girls sought to dispel their body heat and their irrational longing for the night.

"According to Ida Melange," my friend philoso-phized, "darkness is a deep mobile space, which, inhaled through nostrils and eyes, gives primal fullness to things. Making use of spherical geome-try she represents darkness with sensitive graphs, creating a spacial metrics. In my opinion she is wrong, though, because darkness is transient and corruptible."

He added, smiling, that darkness can be found also in the nodes of snails, in butterflies, in the splendor of trumpets.

"Don't you hear the trumpets of the owls?" Yaluna sighed. "They are arriving already."

"How strange," I remarked.

According to Sinus, we could not hear them approaching because these strigidae have soft plumage, so their flight is silent when they take off from the old walls, the belfries, and the rocky cliffs that surround Zebulonia.

Their raucous song spread gradually. I believe it started from the belltower of Santa Maria, nearby, since it sounded metallic, reverberating from the bells. First to respond to that call were the strigi-dae of the countryside, since it was quiet there.

"Take note, Ariete," my friend tried to explain, "they are communicating with each other. They are rousing each other with the sensation of music."

The song from the countryside was audible through the rounding shadows in the trees. During the many years of my absence that species of feathered creature had increased to the detriment of others.

Sinus, quick to complicate everything, said,
"You see, this other language is gradually being
superimposed on that of the peasants. It's a kind of
primitive expressive force based on the consonance
of numbers. In this case, series of them can be
identified that produce harmonies: the hemiolion,
the epitriton, the triplar, the quadruple."*

Some old men were leaning out of the windows,
others had gone out into the street. Pleasing in its
harmony, the hooting of the owls came from San
Pietro, from Itria, from the alleys and little holes in
the walls. Responsive to the dominance of sound,
the women were caressed and excited by it, while
on the contrary the men were beginning to feel
through their bodies the numbness of their hands.

Was Sinus right in saying that in my town the
spiritual universe was being replaced by the
primitive sound of the vibratory vortex?

"Ariete," he said, "men learned to vocalize by
hearing the birds sing in the forest."

"You mean to say that they were our teachers?"

"Exactly. And now the Zebulonians, freeing
themselves from their bodily rhythms, are no longer
subject to snares nor dependent on food."

Around us the old men kept silent. I believe
they were just surfacing to the current of the world,
some with a moan, some with a sigh, some with a
sighing bronchial whistle. They felt themselves
carried on confluent waves of time with crests
distinct from one another. The sounds of the birds
were also emerging from the funereal flows of lava
under the influence of a dull Saturn.

"In the past," Sinus explained, "the Zebulonians
related everything to wheat, to the fava bean, to the
furrow; today they have forgotten all this because

they are immersed in time waves, which we may imagine as cartwheeling yet superindividual electromagnetic entities. That is, for them it's like a river that swallows them and carries them along and lets them float up now and then as surface waves. Am I making myself clear? We could take psychograms to register the intensity, meaning, and direction of the emotions of your people. We are dealing with vector quantities here."

As I followed him sadly, Mario Sinus smiled, saying that science applied the Ida Melange way is meaningless, just as subject to variables as all psychic phenomena. If anything, according to him, one might speak of the effraction by which the past penetrates the present and condenses in it.

Meanwhile in Zebulonia the darkness of night gathered itself in the bodies of spiders and plunged down in indivisible points into the stony fields. Only in the vicinity of Varanna, in the labyrinth of the alleys, did the poorest old women, sitting by their ancient kerosene lamps, make rosaries out of pomegranate seeds or, closing their eyes, pray to the great principle that moves the world.

Since the owls remember their nests and the warm winds of the peaks, their song brought the nocturnal elements into harmony. Ahead of us, Yaluna had taken from the large pocket of her apron an alarm clock of the old round-bellied type with a bell on top where a little lead ball struck a tin cap. By then a softer, quieter sound prevailed among the owls, recalling the color blue.

"They are feminine tones," said the psychiatrist, a connoisseur of the science of rhythms. "Have you noticed that the deeper tones are decreasing?"

Sitting on a step Yaluna was listening to her alarm clock, remembering her lost children and calling them by name. And one's children, we know, can be felt in the joints of one's hands, in a violet, or in a wheeling moment of joy.

Under the deep evening sky, the town rang with sound. That night we made the acquaintance of the boy called Mercurio, an unusual name in Zebulonia, where, in homage to the traditions of our elders, the most common names were Salvatore, Giovanni, Antonio, Giuseppe, Agrippino, Domenico, Sebastiano, Mario, and Maria, Maruzza, Angela, Arcangela, Mena, Riricchia, Vincenza, Ignazina, Agrippina, Yana, Caterina. Names which expressed the ancient borders of a limited onomastic province, never subject to dispersion; their round vowels melodiously suggest a closed family group.

The boy had come with a clarinet into the open space formed by the heaped remains of the destroyed Norman castle.

"Who is he?" I asked Yaluna, but she probably did not hear me, intent as she was on the ticking of her alarm clock and the memories of her children.

The owls of the valley gradually ceased to sing, followed by those inhabiting the peaks and finally by the ones that usually nested in Zebulonia. Sitting on a heap of stones, Mercurio then began to play his silver instrument, delicate tones, which soon turned deeper, evoking sparks and reverberations all around. Through virtuoso passages the sound intertwined with the tendrils rooted in the walls, with the dwarf trees of the roofs, with the magnetic chalcedony. Yaluna awakened from the dream of her children, listened, and said, "Ariete, when you were here we didn't have this custom.

Now, as you see, Mercurio circles the open space here to send the lament of his clarinet in all directions. This way the lemons in the valley make better growth."

As we had seen coming up the slope when we arrived, the lemon groves were not rounded and bushy, but dusty, their pale branches stunted. The fruits were green, with yellow stripes and dark spots.

"Ariete," Yaluna continued, "we old people enjoy it because it is a sound without old age. It lets me breath better, it dispels the phantoms from my soul, it gives me the feeling that all things are fleeting."

"Strigidae and peasants," Sinus told me, "are like biological holes in the night."

"What are you saying?"

"Listen: by accumulating vibrations and magnetic swarms within themselves, they create time."

According to Sinus, time, through people, and in this case through the Zebulonians, stars the endless void with tiny craters like the ones we admire on a perfect lunar map. That is, it is we who cause time to brim over.

The smallest children were sleeping on the ground, the bigger ones were listening to Mercurio, the old men were leaning against their doors. A slanting light fell upon them from street lamps fixed, under a zinc-plated pan, to a tall L-shaped pole, the old-style electric streetlighting of Zebulonia.

27

III

When the owls stopped singing, I wanted to go to my mother Algazèlia.

"Oh, don't you know?" said Yaluna. "She's left."

"Left? At her age?"

"Yes, Ariete. And your Uncle Michele, Tèlefo the swordswallower, Ops the fiddler, Mnémio the blind man, and various peasants, men and women, went with her."

"Why, Yaluna?"

"The town water fountains have dried up. They went to search for water."

"Come," I said to Sinus.

My mother's house, across from the church, was abandoned. The outer door, of brown walnut, was locked. I could not open it, since I no longer had the long iron key with the ring on the end. From outside I looked at the lintel that jutted out over the door in three slabs, capped by a round arch with semioval ribs. Under these a wrought iron lunette in a sun-ray pattern bore the initials, P. S., of the first owner, Patrizio Símili (because her ancestral home was in the Baudanzas' court, in an alley where in spring the sunlight arrived only at midday).

"You should know, Sinus, that beyond the outer door there are two flights of stairs, painted a light color with brown bands. On the first flight there is an earthenware pot on each side. At the top a small walnut door, already splitting."

My friend was listening. So I told him that the house is composed of nine rooms besides the long balcony and two little terraces from which one can follow the rising of the clouds from the Erei Mountains.

Under the balcony that runs around the house there are a wild fig tree and an almond tree; in summertime my mother picks their fruits, tiny but sweet. The walls appear to have been built with stone blocks from the castle destroyed by the earthquake of 1693. If you look carefully, or scrape the limestone – both on the Via Roma side and on the opposite side where the facade displays a small window, a false door and a real door leading into a ground floor room – you can make out the pommels of swords, the remains of sculpted chimeras, fragments of scrolls, one of which reads "What is here is there, what is there is here," that is: sunset is dawn, and the soul of the individual, through the reaping of sycamores and through simple goodness, becomes the Absolute.

"It's too much," my friend sighed. Yaluna, who had followed us, invited us to spend the night at her house. The neighboring church clock struck twelve geometrically ringing signals, which, moving from roof to roof, and, beyond Zebulonia, from crag to crag, told us that life, though short, is beautiful in our potential to create energy and thought. The same hour, in different tones, rang from all the other steeples. As we know, Zebulonia is full of clocks. There are clocks on the steeples, their faces, on which the day blends its flames, visible from a great distance. There are clocks on the corners of the upper streets, some without hands by now. The most common ones are the solar clocks, with a gnomon. They are found, worn by the weather, on rocky spurs, on an outside column of the Church of Santa Maria itself, under the eaves of houses, all registering, in various degrees of intensity, the light of the galaxy Andromeda, or the vivid white light of Jupiter, reminding the Zebulonians that celestial influences are verifiable in the bodies of those who receive them.

That is why the old Zebulonians have lean bodies and a slow but steady step, still wear heavy woolens and dark caps, and say very little. Their gait accentuates the swinging motion of their arms, while their spine remains straight. The women adhere to this model too, and tend to all sorts of daily tasks very capably as well. They are short, and well-proportioned, like my mother Algazèlia, born March 6, 1894, last of twenty-four children, some of whom we name here: Ciccio, Antonio, Turi, Agrippina, Cicciopino, Paolo, Ignazio, Santo, Marannella, Rosilla, Yana, Giovanni, Arriga, Maruzza, Yanuzzu, Tinuzzu, Mario, and Papè (that's my mother). Since my grandfather, Mastro Turi Casaccio,* was a baker, Algazèlia as a girl carried bread to the shops of Zebulonia in a hamper, marking with one or more notches on a stick the quantity she delivered. She carried semolina rolls, the *cucchi* or "twins," which were two joined buns, round loaves, and common rolls called *guastedde*. Because durum wheat was used, the bread was especially crunchy, with a golden color, and a marvelous smell, so that the sparrows, lovers of roofs and of people, would surround her those mornings to peck at the crumbs. At that time there were about ten bakers in my town, among whom my grandfather was celebrated for the graceful shapes of his bread and for the flours he selected, so that he represented an important link in the chain of breads, silks, woven cloths, baskets, sieves that were produced daily. On holy days he was asked to bake the tiny rolls that every family brought to church to be blessed. His breads were of unusual and lovely shapes, formed with a hand like no other. For instance, he made ring-shaped ones with scalloped inner edges, saucer-shaped ones with hardboiled eggs in them, unleavened breads, semolina bread with sesame seeds, or big rye loaves. In his work he had the help of his children, among whom my aunt Agrippina, called Pipí, and her brother Antonio excelled in giving sugary colors and unexpected shapes to the rolls: children's faces, goslings taking flight, St. Sebastian pierced by arrows, mysterious sphinxes, and plowing oxen, which reminded the Zebulonians of the labor and sweetness of living. In people's homes those rolls were placed around the portraits of the dead so they could smell their fragrance in the depths of time that united them in death. In church the priests used them to decorate the patrician chapels where the famous men of Zebulonia were buried. The story goes that my grandfather Turi was inspired by my grandmother, Maria Palermo, to squeeze sweet dough into all sorts of shapes, even lovely fruits adorning baskets made of bread.

As for the breadmaking activity of the average home, on the other hand, it was not unusual to see women handing yeast, or "growth" as it was called, from window to window, or the loaves themselves, baked in special ovens with red hot olive and carob wood. Sometimes the rolls could be found on

balconies, on streetcorners, on rooftops, to satisfy
the hunger of the blackbirds that flocked in from
the countryside. My mother usually crumbled bread
and biscuits on the slopes of the Mura quarter
among nettles and cornflowers to attract goldfinches. She had been born in the St. Agrippina
quarter, in the house of the Barberas, where at night
they lit hanging oil lamps when outside the starry
mantle was spread. There she had acquired a love
for diligent work, for keeping birds in cages, for
seeking treasures among the plants in the walls of
dark cisterns. By crocheting socks and selling the
eggs of her one hen, she managed when she was
about twenty to buy herself a third-class ticket on
the steamer *Madonna,* on which, after a stormy
crossing during which the steamer *Patria* sank, she
reached her sisters and brothers in New York; she
worked in a shirt factory there for four years,
returning at the death of her mother in 1923.

Like the other women of Zebulonia, with her
quick intelligence she brings the aphorisms of her
speech into harmony with the vegetable spirit of
parietarias, squills, and myrrh. A good cook, she
can prepare savory, spicy sauces, pasta with
eggplants, caponata, omelets with fresh fava beans,
salty ricotta, milk dessert, prickly pear and quince
jams in molds shaped like heads, horses, flowers,
branches. She knew various techniques of making
almond paste, which, (I went on with my story to
Sinus), after a good year, the cart drivers used to
buy to resell, coming from all the other towns. On
the main roads at night you could see the lines of
carts with their lamps lit between the wheels.
During the day we boys cracked the big, rounded,
soft-shelled almonds, opening them easily with our

fingers. In all the alleys, women sat on the ground near their doorsteps shelling the other kind of almonds, taking them from special baskets and cracking them with stones. The shells of both sorts were kept to make charcoal to keep warm in the winter. Since the nuts were so abundant, my mother crushed them in a gold mortar (our only precious object) that she had found by chance as a child among the ruins of the town of Trinacia, on Mt. Catalfaro where my grandfather Casaccio owned a piece of land. The other women crushed them in chopping bowls of bronze, or onyx, or zinc, their concave base reinforced with porphyry. All sorts of things were made with ground almonds: for instance, tied in muslin handkerchiefs, it was put to soak in water drawn from certain olive springs, that is, springs that rose in olive groves, or from under rocks on the lower slopes of the mountains. Thus almond milk was obtained, white, translucent, delicious to palate and nostrils. It was believed to strengthen the memory and purify the boundless extension of all the passions. Buns were also flavored with it, as well as dumplings that my mother baked slowly in the oven with roots of thyme and bayleaves from the valley. Sweetened with honey, they were eaten to celebrate the full moon that rose slowly from the lowlands silvering the eyes of us children. It was a great joy for us and for everybody, because there was no electric light in Zebulonia then and everyone knew that the oil lamps were to be lit only when strictly necessary. The poorest families rejoiced in the disappearance of the darkness, eating sweet lemons and the reddish kind whose delicious juice was sucked very slowly. My mother would tell us five children to stare at the moon steadily in order to gather in through our pupils its infinite particles, which would come swirling like pebbles to fill our hearts, and to store them for when the sulphurous new moon returned.

While I was recounting all this to Sinus, Yaluna said, "Ariete, what are you telling your friend the professor? Those times are over. There is nothing left. Even the richness of our olives is gone, the trees are decaying, withering, sparrows and partridges find no refuge in them any more. Fortunately, before Dolcissimo disappeared, perhaps because of the fate of his daughter 'Alqama, he used to bring us fragrant herbs from the countryside. So I got the idea of making oil from basil, oregano, and bitter rue. You can also put in cinnamon, or, if you want it stronger, a pinch of cubeb, rare plants in our region, cultivated by Dolcissimo among rocks where warm winds blow."

Sinus became curious about this person and asked my townswoman if she could arrange a meeting with him.

"I already told you," she answered, "he hasn't been seen lately. He's been gone ever since his daughter 'Alqama hasn't been herself."

"Would it be possible to meet 'Alqama?" Mario Sinus pressed.

Yaluna made a vague gesture, so full of apprehension that it dissuaded the psychiatrist. As the woman went on about oils that could be extracted from orange blossoms, lemons, saffron, he observed to me that the fragrances of the countryside have neither form nor rest because the great heat diffuses them, subtle, clement, and excitable, from plants and herbs.

"Stop talking about these things," Yaluna sighed. "Come to my house. You can spend the night there if you are willing to make do with what I have."

We followed her through a narrow alley that led to the Mura quarter where the houses, on the fairly steep slope looking southwest, were all closed up.

"How come?" I asked. "Because it's late?"

"Oh no, Ariete. Only I and Angelina Saudano, with whom you used to play as a boy, live here now."

We stopped. I explained to Mario Sinus that in that outlying section defensive walls had stood in the past, since Zebulonia, because of its location, had been a fortress. I added that Michele Amari in his history of the Moslems tells us that the Saracens defeated in 829 by the Byzantine Theodotus, when their young leader Ased the Invader died, took refuge in Zebulonia and, close to starvation, ate donkeys and mules. As luck would have it, a small fleet of Spanish Moslems came sailing along the coast of Sicily and went to the help of their brethren besieged in Zebulonia. On their way they enriched themselves with the silver coins called *dirhem abbàssidi* on which kufic inscriptions reminded the faithful that Allâh by his manifest greatness radiates from the inner soul of things.

Amari writes: "It was during the heat waves of July and August in the year 830 that the army of Asbagh, a strange compound of marauders, heroes, conquerors, and saints, surrounded the Byzantine troops of Theodotus at the foot of the mountain of Zebulonia. The Byzantines were left without water, the Spanish Berbers having diverted certain streams in the vicinity of the copper district.

Skilled in the art of war, the Berbers, having cast into the favorable wind powders of lead and black stone, and minute fragments of emeralds and rubies, attacked the enemy army, routing it and killing Theodotus himself. As the solar streams of the desert were setting the approaching evening ablaze, they burst into Zebulonia, tearing down the walls, burning its olive trees, and putting to the sword every man they encountered. When the moon rose, brimful of her daily journey, oval and distended above the flaming roofs, those who were not lying with a woman thanked Allâh, the merciful, the compassionate, who had helped them with his swift hand. Afterward, Asbagh marched with his entire army against a town that Baiân spells Ghalûlia or Ghallûlia, which – from the sound of its name – would seem to be the Calloniana of the Itinerary of Antonino, located not far from the Salso, which, dragging shields, seven-layered breastplates, shinguards, and dead Capricorn horses brought by Ased as well as Asbagh, flows towards the waters of the sea."*

"From those unions, Sinus," I concluded, "a race was born that is still predominant in my town. The inhabitants, as you have seen, are rather short, averaging 1.63 meters in height, with black hair, rarely kinky. They hark to the three-fold sound that comes from the gullets of men, from roosters, and from stones that ring like lyres when the thunder booms."

"But why," Yaluna wailed, "are you telling all these secret stories of ours?"

Bats flew around us. Stellar neutrons and mesons rushed down on us. Mario Sinus asked that we take a look at some of those abandoned homes. "Our inquiry must be complete," he said.

He crossed a kitchen garden covered with dung so dry it seemed concrete. Beyond it there was a gallery to which we climbed with some difficulty because it had been taken over by so-called mayflowers, which are really the *chrysanthemum segetum* of high cliffs. Several generations of them had overtaken each other, and the bushes had grown tall enough to reach the crumbling balcony.

"But Ariete," Yaluna complained, "why do you insist on visiting a house where nobody lives? Doesn't it seem to you an offense to the Salemi family, which doesn't exist any more?"

We did not listen to her. Pushing our way through, we saw that the door had been eroded by those enormous flowers, most of them dried up now, which in the blindness of their intense growth had occupied the only room of the small building. Reaching upward, those floral shoots had almost totally hidden the poor furniture: a chest of drawers, three chairs, a bed. We advanced, pushing aside those chrysanthemums, and, lighting a lamp, saw insects, long dead, crumbling to powder and falling to the floor, earwigs and hornets. Geckos clustered on the rafters.

"What kingdom have we come to?" Sinus wondered, shielding his face from the huge swaying flowers that climbed the walls.

IV

We accepted Yaluna's hospitality. She lived in the
Mura quarter, in a two-room ground floor shed.
She was so glad to have us that she lit the kerosene
lamp. Hanging on the walls from strings we saw a
sieve, a hoe, branches of orange, two large ceramic
dishes with a blue background on which were painted an ox, Hope as a beautiful woman, and, expressing wonder and pleasure, a young king holding a
book of sophistries. As is the custom among our
peasants who cannot afford sufficient living space,
strings of dried figs, a bread basket, a jug of fresh
cool water, and bunches of azaroles were hanging
from the wooden rafters. The mattresses were
stuffed with straw, with a snow-white cover on
which with her own hands our friend had embroidered the earthly paradise – rose-colored trees
whose very trunks were heavy with round fruits,
under which rivers of a thousand colors ran.

"Did you make this?" Sinus asked her.

"That's right. When they were little my children
would ask me, in winter, when they couldn't stay
out in the fields, 'Mother, what is paradise? Where
is it?' So I made it to make them happy."

We slept blissfully. Toward morning we were
awakened by the roosters and the narrow bands of
light that fell on the picture before us, called
"Time," a cheap print often seen in Zebulonian
homes. It depicts a double flight of stairs, ascending and descending. On every step there is a

38

man who progresses from infant to adult, a hunter, a father with children, then grows gray at the temples and bent with age. "Thus is our life," it reads, "which twists and turns from bright to dark, and vanishes."

"Good morning," said Yaluna, who had slept in the next room that had a dirt floor without bricks. "I have made you some hydromel, which 'Alqama is very fond of too. Drink it. It sharpens the eyesight and allows us to hear the sounds that roots emit when they die of too much sun. Drink it."

"Give us your blessing," I said spontaneously, remembering the ancient salutation of my townspeople who favor a terse simplicity.

When we were outside, Sinus asked, "How come there are so many roosters crowing?" And in fact, on the roofs of the abandoned shacks, among the yellow locust trees of the slope, on the thresholds colored by the rising sun, and even down in the almond trees of Sei Canali, there were roosters, their wings outstretched and their throats turned to the east.

"My sons," the old woman answered, "who do you expect to take care of these creatures any more? They reproduce on their own, with no owner, they feed on seeds, leaves, scarabs."

They went on crowing.

"Why don't you take us to 'Alqama?" my friend proposed. "The more people we see, the better our book will be."

"Ahh," the old woman sighed. "It seems right to me that that girl be left to her destiny."

Perhaps to distract us, the woman began to scratch in the ground in front of her house where in the reddish earth she had planted a crocus that

39

looked half-dead to me, a mottled broom, a licorice plant with black streaks.

"See," she said, "since I can't chase around the countryside, I raise these plants here."

"Why don't you introduce us to 'Alqama?" Sinus repeated.

"All right," the woman said. "But remember that the crocus, the licorice plant, and the broom have a sweet smell for the nose, flavor for the palate, and light for the eye, while 'Alqama, poor child, offers none of them."

We took the path of the night before. Yaluna went ahead of us bringing a basket for 'Alqama with small apples very pale near the stem, some honey, a few sprays of mallow in bloom, and a chunk of sulphur.

"She'll be glad, you'll see," she said. "She's always alone and few people seek her out." Iacò Lane was empty; no one was to be seen.

"The Gate of Bacchus," I told Sinus, "once stood here, corrupted to 'Iacò.' Since this spur of the mountain was full of vineyards that went all the way down to the valley, Bacchus was honored here by eating grapes and pressing their juices. Throughout October there was singing; the poets that Zebulonia is renowned for enjoyed themselves improvising jocular verses, madrigals, and sonnets."

"I don't remember that," Yaluna interjected. "I only remember the grape arbors that went up to the roofs in this street."

From the open space at the castle, we could see those roofs below us. Mario Sinus counted up to eight hundred and twenty-seven, extending among ruins and sandpits from the north round to the west

40

and petering out towards the break in the hills to the east.

"We can see the whole town from here," the psychiatrist smiled. "We can circumscribe it with three lines that make up a sort of equilateral triangle. The first nucleus grew around this height, which was originally a fortress."

"That's right, Sinus."

"Let's trace it geometrically."

"Oh, listen," I went on, "one line goes through the Church of Santa Maria, which was once the Temple of the Sun, from which two lion-shaped rocks remain in front of the main entrance. The other angle is to be found at the belltower of San Pietro on our left. The last angle fits perfectly in the sheared-off tower of the Church of Santa Agrippina."

"That is," my friend went on while Yaluna offered us some apples, "the first Zebulonians huddled behind this height so as not to see its ascending form, which lifted their minds to the celestial vortex."

Ibn Zafèr writes: "In their divine wisdom, out of the triangle through which they created a relationship with the cardinal points, the Zebulonians left free the view of the valleys below and the Erei Mountains beyond. Thus they felt at ease with themselves, with their predisposition to invent stories, their soft hearts swimming in wild desires. Witness the way their dwellings hug each other, the sharp incline of their roofs, their preference for limestone, from which, if rainfall is abundant, the flower of the lul-daghelí may suddenly sprout."

"Have you gotten lost in the view there?" Yaluna admonished us. "How do you know Ibn

Zafèr? They say he was a prophet who fought against the insolent and the proud, and against the race of the giants. Come, don't you know that 'Alqama lives in that house just below the castle?"

The young woman did not want to open the door.

"Don't worry," our friend said, "I know these people. One is Ariete, the son of Don Nanè, the tailor. You were just a baby when he was our doctor twenty years ago."

In the doorway the parietaria grew even out of a crack from which a pomegranate thrust its first tender shoots. In that two-room dwelling we saw the strangest objects: ears of wheat, tin foil, wings of cabbage butterflies, powders that vanished as you looked at them, withered roses, bunches of oregano, a little bag of pepper, bits of glass, curls of cinnamon. 'Alqama, who wore a brocade gown, stared at us in a reverie. She had a cream perfumed with thyme on her hands.

"She uses it," the old woman told us softly, "to propitiate her dreams."

To Sinus it seemed that the young woman was living in an inexplorable hiatus in the world. Hanging from the rafters of the second room by cords of agave were five cages, in them a sparrow, a finch, a blackbird, a partridge, a robin. Sinus, searching for the spiritual meaning of the objects, explained to me in gestures and murmurs that the young woman was living in a fugitive state of becoming because she believed that she was moving back and forth between her body and an extracorporeal zone where she imagined her life was throbbing.

"Her notion of time is upset," he opined, "because events thicken around her without a future."

42

The case interested Mario Sinus greatly, for he saw in the young woman one of the focal points of our inquiry: the center of the circle, the model of perfect balance in contrast to human imbalance, the flame of our countless loves. According to my friend, in 'Alqama the mind of the Zebulonians, the sensitive soul of plants, the qualities of air and water converged.

So he asked that we study her, with the help of Yaluna. On the second day we noticed that the girl drew light from everything, near or far. Of the rays that beat at the window she – how shall I say it? – captured both the less brilliant, peripheral ones and the brighter middle ones. She received us unwillingly because she was afraid that in our presence her hands would gather from the infinite perizebulonian space the deep red of the poppies, the blue of the olive trees, or the green of the sheepgrass. Since in her the silent nature of the Zebulonian women was accompanied by evident mental dissociation, my friend tried to help her express herself with dots, nonsense morphemes, outlines of real objects. He also made use of a series of concentric circles.

"Through these clues," the ethnopsychiatrist explained, "we shall interpret her thought and find a key to understanding the present world of your townspeople."

But she interacted with the environment through graceful movements of her fingers and limbs that became quite complex in a few days: very subtle movements of her fingertips seeming to animate the room, the muscles of her forearms flowing, the tips of her feet tracing oneiric designs.

It is well known, my brother Timor, that electrons around the nucleus, planetary orbits around the sun, the reciprocal spiraling of almond flowers make such movements, all expressing a sameness of numbers. And numbers, remember, were what Ida Melange and Mario Sinus were all too fond of, although from a different point of view. In *De amore mutatis mutandis,* the former was looking for a relationship between mental tensions and numbers, applying the principles of a Pythagorean primitivism; the latter saw in them living events observable in both the physical world and in the human mind. According to my friend, numbers were involved in breathing, in trees, in voices, in the ticking of a clock. With a glint in his eyes that frightened me, he told me that the body of the young woman measured, according to his calculations, two hundred seventy seconds in height, and fifty-seven in width. That is, he was trying to determine the possibility of objectifying the pulsations of the universe through numbers.

Gradually, following our suggestions, 'Alqama began to draw on the walls, on the inside lintels of the two windows and the balcony, on her own body, more than on paper. It was certainly in memory of her departed father that she sketched tiny little birds, some of a leaden color, others saffron, or flaming red. Their wings were delicate or heavy with tears, some barely visible against leafy patterns. Most were spread wide, the rowing feathers vermilion (down to their roots), or immersed in terrestrial rivers.

All this could be explained by the last occupation of Dolcissimo, 'Alqama's father, who had been a birdcatcher, and by the abundance of

birds that in the past were to be seen around
Zebulonia. In the lower districts, near open country, the piercing song of sparrows was heard.
Along the paths one came upon blackbirds – not
being talkative, they sat in the mulberry trees
enjoying the vapors rising from the valleys, or the
mountain nymphs. Zebulonian birds hardly ever
move in great flocks, favoring a low, silent flight,
mostly through the olive groves.

The girl preferred robins and blackbirds because
they love the berries of cool places and the proxim-
ity of river banks. She also painted downy grasses,
ferns, and daphnes. The things that most amazed us
was the discovery of hundreds of dolls in the attic.
There were dolls made of silk, of woven papyrus, of
laurel leaves, of moonstones, of sugar, of sugar
cane. They had eyes that could move, and mouths
that could sing. They had been arranged along the
walls at the points where the hours had their
luminous center, so that they could make the most
of the passing of the day, and collect its most
delicate elements. For instance, in some of them
the eyes were prisms that reflected light as they
rolled slowly; in others the passage of the sun
turned indigo in the reflected rays; in one row the
first dark signs of evening gathered among the pale
blue lights of their cheeks. There were dolls in
Arabic dress, with dark ringlets and fake tiaras; in
Norman dress, blond, lost in wonder at themselves
and their surroundings; Spanish style, sumptuously
dressed in taffeta, with castanets, giving off heavy
odors. Two dolls resembled Christian saints, in
prayer, exalting the wondrous eternals of life and
death. For accessories there were buckles, tiny

scarves, shawls, scowling servants, systoles and diastoles of the world.

To complete the picture of her family we must reconstruct the figure of Dolcissimo.

"Oh, tell us about him," Sinus pleaded with Yaluna.

"But how many things do you people want to know! We Zebulonians are on one side and everybody else on the other. Why do you want to do all that digging into our past?"

We got to know many things about the man by asking old people, boys, women, Yaluna, the very wind that sometimes brought us his voice. I helped the psychiatrist a good deal with my own memories. Dolcissimo was not taller than five feet five, thin, much given to meditation and sadness as well as to laughter. He observed closely the aggregation and the separation of the natural elements that caught his attention. As a young man he often visited the house of my paternal grandmother, Donna Cecè, who had seven children – my father Settimo Emanuele, Pino, Ignazina, Peppino, Tatò Carmelo (called Tutú), and Gino. They lived in Vespri Square, and the ground floor of their house was the shop of my grandfather Papè, who was a butcher. From towns and villages, from castles and monasteries, there arrived at that shop sellers of artichokes, eggplants, honey, pitchers, flasks, discarded religious vestments, equinoctial fruits, wines, and finally of rosary beads and small crucifixes carved out of elephant tusks. Friars came too, who went around preaching a mixture of Gospel and Koran as well as the death that rises from the sea; and in exchange for a night spent in the straw among mules and donkeys they left my uncles and aunts prayer books, St. Augustine's *The City of God,* Apuleius' *On Magic,* Passavanti's *Mirror of True Penitence,* Fazio degli Uberti's *Dittamondo,* and *Picatrix* by the great Arab sorcerer Albumasar. These books were stored by my relatives in a chest made with panels from carts on which scenes of the French Paladins were painted.* I told Mario Sinus that among these books I remembered the novels of Carolina Invernizio and Hugo, Andrea da Barberino's *Guerin Meschino,* Goethe's *Voyage to Italy,* the *Fragments* of Empedocles' *On Nature,* and a rare text by the physicist Aristarchos of Samos, who back in the third century before Christ, besides devising the sundial, had the intuition that our earth is pulled around the sun by sesquialternate chords played by lunar winds.

Dolcissimo knew all these books, but he was particularly entranced by *The Sizes and Distances of the Sun and the Moon* by the above-mentioned Aristarchos, and even more by the three editions of *The Arabian Nights:* one with a cover perfumed with gum benjamin, illustrated with scimitars that cut it in two; a second one that changed color from page to page according to the events, the dreams, the wars being waged: pale if the traveler was caught up in some enchantment, vermilion if war was predominant, aquamarine if vain illusions of love were the subject. The third edition, kept in a box with corners of green gold, was trilingual: Arabic, Spanish, and Sicilian, written in minute characters with jade filigree.

To fill the idle hours of winter evenings, these people who came from every corner of the island brought in their carts, together with their goods, guitars, mandolins, and even a violin. The art of playing instruments, already cultivated in the family of my grandmother Cecè, increased in those years.

Thus Dolcissimo learned to strum peasant lullabies, folksongs, mournful ballads, songs of the outlaws, theogonies illustrating the emergence of gods from rivers and mountain crevices.

Dolcissimo spent a good deal of time in the artisans' shops. The shoemakers were grouped, for the most part, as we have said, in hovels and real caves in the Itria quarter. They knew all there was to know about every sort of twine, leathers, cobbling knives, but accustomed as they were to thinking about the moon that came to visit their benches, they had become storytellers who knew that it is the air that makes the seedbed sprout and that our flat earth sails on a vast ocean. The barber shops were located in Buglio Square, at the center of town, or very close to the square in the streets radiating from it. They were rectangular in shape, with four swivel chairs having no mirrors in front of them, and they threw the shadows of the peasants gathered there on the faded walls. These places had a curious relationship to the tailor shops: if an imaginary line were drawn from the back of every barber shop it would end up in a tailor shop.

"Dolcissimo," Yaluna said, "went to his friends the barbers in the winter because it was warm there. And there he heard talk about fallow land, November rain, plants that preserve sap in their roots."

His relationship to the tailors was different, because these men, concentrating their eye on the needle and thread, altered common opinions by means of their unique mental processes. They knew the origin of whatever is subtle; they created symbols for the chimerical; from their stools they followed the movement of the day across the roofs; they knew intuitively that the feet of the world were immersed in the spinning vortex. From these craftsmen Dolcissimo had learned new desires, a flair for the imaginary, the tendency to dream, moods and fears about the passing of time.

Sinus classified the man as schizoid and placed him on the chart of the various types of Zebulonians he was gradually drafting.

Dolcissimo, following the instructions of the travellers who were put up between the mules and the hay in the shop of my paternal grandfather, had made himself two guitars, perhaps to gratify his soul. One was made of wild rosewood, the other of eucalyptus. Gradually the custom arose for him to meet with the old and the blind. The latter came from the Centímolo quarter, one behind the other, finding their way with the bamboo canes in their hands. And you know, my brother Timor, that patches of bamboo abound in our region, on steep slopes, in ravines, and around houses. They are useful as material for hampers, breadbaskets, roofing lath, trays on which figs and split tomatoes are dried during the summer. They have singing leaves and hollow conduits through which one can hear the breath of the wind gurgling, if they have been carefully cut.

"Oh Dolcissimo," the blind men would call. "Are you in front of Don Papè's shop?"

They surrounded him trying to discern his shape with the feeble light of their corneas.

"We are here," one would say. "Will you talk to us about olive trees this morning?"

"Talking" for them meant playing, Yaluna continued. Dolcissimo plucked his rosewood guitar, drawing from it a folk tune that seemed gradually to fade into sleep over the waters of the trickling brooks.

"Oh," the blind men would say, "don't you hear the olive trees rustling?"

Another would ask, "Tell us about fava beans."

They were a substitute for bread. The peasants ate them fresh, fried with eggs in omelettes, as well as dried, cooked whole and eaten using onion leaves as spoons. They were also consumed skinned and mashed, in a coarse mixture with olive oil and flour.

The guitar was gentle now, as if to give sensory properties to the imagined fava beans. The old people could feel its mild rhythm on their lashes.

"Now tell us about Fiumecaldo," another blind man begged.

"All right," Dolcissimo would say.

He would take the eucalyptus guitar and rouse its voice with his fingers and a tin pick in studied measures, even, odd, and odd-even. One heard a kind of flowing of waters, a mournful melody that brightened when Dolcissimo plucked the rosewood guitar again to combine the vibrations of the two. The old men compensated for their lack of the visual with the aural, their memory swollen and ailing. They did not know that the sterility of the soil of Zebulonia was absolute, now that, among other things, the olive trees had been destroyed by hypocrisy, deceit, and bad weather. If women went by with their black shawls over their heads, they walked quickly, not to be troubled by that sound.

Since it was daytime and the advancing sun flashed on the eaves and its refraction touched the eyeballs of the old men, they would ask: "Oh, is the sun rising? Is it light already? Is it burning?" Or: "Is it going to be hot? Can you see it on top of the Collegiate Church? If we move will we feel it better on our hands?"

To Sinus the sunlight is the sense of touch itself, which allows us to feel it in oscillating photons that spread through the air from the heavenly circles and reach us thanks to the receptive properties of our retina. Lacking the use of the latter, those Zebulonians felt the sunlight in what ocular membranes they had left and in the crossroads of their hearts. They would ask Dolcissimo to translate the light for them so they could again appreciate its points, its shapes, its cheerfulness.

Thus sound became a complex relationship of tiny intervals: the rosewood sound was sloth of memory or remorse alternating with lust; the eucalyptus sound produced spherical musical particles more rounded at their ends, recalling waters, chasms, and discordant whistling.

Hearing this story, Mario Sinus explained that Dolcissimo, sharpening the senses of the old men, had turned them into forces of the original chaos, in which small things expand to occupy immensity, and fava bean flowers in their cycle become one with the universe.

In the fall Don Mariddu the puppeteer came to Zebulonia from the coastal towns, since it was the season of the olive harvest. For his stories, which he altered at times, adding new parts, he followed *The French Paladins* by Lodico and the book by Pietro Manzaneres published in 1510 in Palermo by Pedone Lauriel. The puppeteer owned the *Guerin Meschino* in the 1473 Paduan edition by the publisher Valdezochio, the *Cantar de mi Cid,* and the *Chanson de Roland.* It seems that Dolcissimo played the guitar on those evenings, and my uncle Pino the violin, at the foot of the stage on which Don Mariddu, manipulating arms and strings, told the spectators of the ten thousand rivers that flow downstream into the black earth where death is a maiden garlanded with ivy. The sound of the instruments and the flashing of swords favored the rising of the wind abroad in Zebulonia that darkened the empty streets.

Don Mariddu owned seven hundred and twenty scenes painted on cardboard and the paper in which sugar was wrapped, that on Sundays, with the help of his children and us boys, he displayed on street corners, in the square, on the arches of the Adinolfo Gate, on patrician balconies. The town was red with autumnal forests, paladins, sendals, ladies' white shoulders, tents adorned with the horns of the crescent.

If it was raining very hard, the vendors would remain seated on the straw in my grandfather's shop listening to Dolcissimo read *The Arabian Nights.* Or they looked at the marionettes that my Uncle Carmelo, called Tutú, had made in the carpenter shop of Don Gisimo Leone. There were twelve of them, carved out of carob wood (later he gave them to me, and I kept them hidden in the lean-to next to Rondello, our donkey): Charlemagne with a purple mantle, Roland with a copper Durendal, Roger riding the Hippogryph, Bradamant with her head weighed down by bellicose thoughts, the pensive Oliver, Ganelon de Mayence with a horn on the nape of his neck, the giant Sacripant, a slaughtered Saracen, Medoro with his head carved in the shape of a desert rose, Angelica whose hair gleamed with mercury sulphide.

The guests soaked up rain, memories, and the marionettes' speeches with their eyes, while my grandmother Cecè to cheer them up sent out dried sausages, homemade salami, slices of pork, that she kept hanging from big nails and pegs in a back room. If the cartdrivers' hands were full of melancholy because of the rain that fell in a million filaments outside in the square, my aunt Ignazina would prepare *angels' hair,* a Spanish sweet she had been taught to make by the nuns. She took one hundred egg yolks, beat them with the left hand to allow the heart's emanations to flow into them, and after having gently greased the bottom of a pan with olive oil, she poured in a very thin layer, tossing it very rapidly over a low flame, then laying it, paper thin, on a slab of pink marble. She rolled them up, cut them with an alabaster knife, and immediately glazed them with cinnamon-flavored honey or chocolate or infusions of rose petals. In the shop the guests ate them silently, listening to Dolcissimo, or following the movements of the marionettes of my young Uncle Tutú.

"Dolcissimo helped us," Yaluna told us, "when there was malaria around."

It came up from the plains in the rainy season, up through the valleys where the wild goats searched for plants to increase their milk. The children felt its arrival through a certain motion of the air that darkened the moon just then taking shape over the rooftops.

"It's coming, it's coming," they shouted.

We tried to escape it by wrapping ourselves in sheets, or by catching as much of the lunar ocean as possible in our hands. The women, my mother Algazèlia among them, even tried to ward it off with the fumes of tiny heads of hornets and cinnamon bark. The peasants fired their old muzzle-loading guns and their thunder dissolved the evil vapors for a time. But it was all useless. The fever, preceded by terrible shivering, disrupted the daily work of the farms. The malaria institute in Càtana, directed by a former student of Grassi, never failed to register between three and six thousand cases of malaria in my town every year. As evening approached all were seized by a dark dread of the sickness, which emerged from caves and ravines like a distant fear. With lamps lit the women went to the homes of their sick neighbors, encouraging them with propitiatory words and channeling the glimmer of the stars into their hovels.

Dolcissimo, still young then (we were listening to Yaluna in silence) used to go to the Trezzito district, where the last patch of oaks stretched in the direction of the plateau of Timucah. There were two cinchona trees there, the red kind known as succirubra. They had been imported by Michelangelo Buglio, brother of the Lodovico who had disseminated Thomism and Copernican heliocentrism in China. The adventurous Michelangelo left his brother in Chinese territory and reached the Peruvian coast in a galleon. Ibn Zafèr informs us: "There, with an almanac in enoplian verses,* he gained the sympathy of Countess Cin-Chon, wife of the viceroy, who was very knowledgeable about the antimalarial virtues of quinine. Michelangelo was the first to import that tree into Europe, by hiding it with potatoes and prickly pears in the hold of a huge boat with which he attempted the return voyage, haunted by the memory of Zebulonia and the faculties of its ancient trees. The Zebulonians cultivated the cinchona so extensively that they supplied the entire island with the bark.

"Sinus," I said, "these trees were neglected when the government brought quinine here."

But the Zebulonians, secretly, so as not to incur penalties for unlawfully cultivating the cinchona, left some of them on the higher reaches of the valley of the Trezzito. The bark infusion, which the old women continued to make secretly in their lean-tos, was more highly valued. Dolcissimo was the liaison between those women and the healing trees, which through the strength of their chemical components burned the plasmodia that reproduced in the blood. The Zebulonian poets who had been cured of malaria usually came to those trees looking for inspiration. Through their feverish thirst and the obstruction of their spleen they had experienced wonderful visions and, shivering and sweating, had sharpened the geometry of their words.

Thus Dolcissimo got into the habit of frequenting country lanes, olive groves, blanched river banks where the eggsacks of the dragonflies were developing. To earn a living he collected fennel, chicory, dandelion, which he sold in town. The peasants who had remained, after the emigration of the younger ones, did not care much for the aromatic plants, but gradually, with Dolcissimo's help, they learned to appreciate them. Between 'Alqama's father and those aromatic herbs a loving relationship existed, due to the tiny shade they cast in the heat of noon or to their warm nature that he assimilated through his fingers from the very gravel where they grew, and a practical relationship as well, because gradually the demand for them grew in the nearby towns. He came to know the places where the squills grew, their flowers rising on straight stems from the thirsty ground. The same was true for oregano, mandrake, cinnamon, which he helped to spread, because they were already becoming rare.

When 'Alqama was a little older she followed her father on these excursions.

"He took her along at the break of day," Yaluna told us, "with Polieno."

"Who was Polieno?" the psychiatrist asked.

"Oh you don't know about him? He was a wise rooster who had taken to warning Dolcissimo with his crowing if something strange was in sight."

From what we could gather, Polieno, by sensing low radioactive currents, was able to distinguish the exact places, the soils and sands that contained the seeds, fibers, and roots of unusual trees. Eventually, Dolcissimo experienced every thought in relation to the soil and the subsoil; he had become attuned, that is, to the stony element from below. He was an earthy temperament, in that he loved to sink his hands in the hot soil and to stretch out in ditches to feel surrounded by tendrils and roots. His daughter, on the other hand, was attracted by things that grow upward, like, for example, the fragrant flower of the almond tree, the branches of the quince, the sunflower, whole fields of which they found (cultivated for their edible seeds), through which she walked to gather the images that flow to the pupil from above.

Since Dolcissimo encouraged the old folks to prize aromatic herbs that keep food from spoiling, bread was consumed warm, spread with oil, pepper and salt; sausages were filled with caciocavallo, wild fennel, red cayenne pepper. They were roasted on grills with wood of cinnamon and laurel.

Since the appearance and strength of our bodies depend on what we eat, Sinus observed in his notes that the Zebulonians ate more sweets than meat.

"Sweets," my friend explained while we walked on the heights of the castle from which, in the distance, one could see the antennae of the Exxon Company, "make the skin more resistant to the rays of the sun; favoring mildness, they open the intellect to the soul of the world."

Zebulonia is cited with regard to the art of confectionery in the *De re coquinaria** of Apicius, who is of the opinion that the best ingredient is its honey, which the bees get from the variety of flowers on its rocky slopes. According to Apicius, Zebulonia has a glutinous honey that sticks to the palate; a light honey that brings subtlety to the unborn through the umbilical vein; a fragrant honey that the seductive bee with her loving play readies in the combs. In the past, in my town, the experts in sweets were the nuns of the seven convents. There, after evening prayers, they mixed ricotta and honey, chose flours from different kinds of wheat, interlaced sugared almonds with pistachio. These sweets were eaten in all the convents of the nearby towns, Ochiolà, Burchiaturo, Kalàt-Yeròn, Plaza Hermosa, Palíca. The friars sent peasants who carried the sweets back in baskets covered with cloths of byssus. To make the beggars happy the nuns handed them sweets through the grating, spiced cakes, ring-shaped biscuits, spumoni, fruitcakes, nougat, quince preserves, buns soaked in pink syrup and topped with chocolate. On important feast days they made angels' hair – my Aunt Ignazina had learned the technique of preparing it from Spanish nuns – and handed it out through the iron grates on clay dishes. The boys, never satisfied, followed the little monks* who came from these towns. They positioned themselves on ridges or in terraced fields to breathe in the sweet breezes those make-believe monks left behind. The consumption of sweets inevitably induced the convents to abandon their rigid theological view of life and yield to the splendors of the imagination, to gentleness, and to the appreciation of physical beauty.

By disseminating his aromatic herbs, Dolcissimo introduced into this ancient culinary civilization a cure for the fears, calamities, and nightmares the people of his town were beginning to experience. Thus rue, which in the past had been a vermifuge, was now combined with wine to give relief from depression. The vapors of mint sedated hunger and the luminous swaying of the autumnal *inula viscosa* calmed anxieties.

'Alqama, who went along with her father and Polieno the rooster, attained a remarkable level of mental abstraction, losing herself in her pursuit of the spirit of the sunflowers. As I said, these plants were cultivated where the sunlight thickened on fields that looked eastward: their yellow color and the circular arrangement of their petals made you want to walk among them. Since olive trees were scarce, the sunflower gave the Zebulonians an oil so delicate it mellowed every dish. Walking from place to place, through deep valleys, saline fields, blazing solitudes, the girl lost her mental balance.

"Unfortunately," Sinus observed, bathed in the sunset that gilded the roofs below, "'Alqama waned, she turned inward, and it couldn't have turned out otherwise, since all around her Zebulonia was falling apart."

Aware of his daughter's illness, Dolcissimo, despondent, would leave before dawn for the ravines and stone pits with his rooster Polieno whose crowing announced the fleeting nature of things. His friends became the country lanes, which, as the town was built on a mountaintop, had been carved out by streams of winter rain and the plodding of mules and donkeys. They were fairly wide, level with the fields into which they drained easily, their alluvial bed edged on both sides by blackberry bushes, wild roses, and hawthorn.

"Even their lanes," the psychiatrist was saying, "may reveal the predispositions of the Zebulonians."

From the heights of the castle I looked with new eyes at those paths that climbed the mountain slopes, winding through earth eroded by rain or sleet, an unbroken white circling around ledges and tufa. Dolcissimo must have enjoyed walking them, with the flowering legumes and clover blooming in the surrounding fields, and the vineyards visible below, bordered by rows of stones and soft stands of wheat.

The man would walk farther and farther, thirty, sixty, a hundred thousand paces, enjoying the glitter of the clay and copper that in some places on that desolate heath were very visible. Indirectly he passed on his distress at the withdrawal of his daughter to the peasants. In town the consumption of the aromatic herbs he brought home increased, but it distorted people's minds with strange visions. We understood what Yaluna had said: "He consoled his daughter by bringing her nestsful of blackcaps and goldfinches. He hid them inside his shirt to warm the featherless birds. But he interfered with nidification. The feathered things left the banks of streams and thick stands of wheat. They even changed the shape of their nests. Some nests were seen cemented with black soot and copper powder. In the stony Nicchiara quarter nests were built that opened downward and the foxes had an easy time grabbing the little birds. It was then the owls left the countryside and went to live on the roofs, the crumbling walls, and the bell towers of Zebulonia.

We realized that 'Alqama and Dolcissimo had become two key elements in the possible interpretation of the new condition of my hometown. At any rate, in his wanderings the man occasionally stopped on the banks of the Fiumecaldo where, it was said, the god of the poor was hiding. This was a power that favored humility and an animistic conception of nature and protected waters and roots. The Zebulonians believe that everything is subject to two contrary forces, that is, the evil spirits, which our oldest folks called *nnonni* if they were male, or *làmie* if female; in the so-called hot hours of the afternoon they may issue from walnut trees, ponds, abandoned wells, cisterns, and during the night from holes in the rocks, even from the whistling wind, or the hands of witches who summon them through mysterious powers. They bring sickness and paralysis, twist tufts of hair, cause sudden voices of undetermined origin to be heard, provoke unfortunate events. They have taught people to evoke demons, to lie, to commit treacherous murders, to gain knowledge of time, destroyer of all existing things. The god of the poor instead, whenever he succeeded in following the course of the sun that runs overhead along the Fiumecaldo, where the axis of the world surfaces, was able to help people to comprehend the science of birds, the ceremonies of purification, and the rites of the dead.

According to Sinus, he was an arboreal divinity, not begotten but emanating from the roots tunneling and branching everywhere through the earth of Zebulonia. We do not know whether Dolcissimo, despite the repeated "Oh yes, oh yes," of our friend Yaluna, believed in the existence of this little god, who was thought of by the peasants as grassy, windy, of changeable aspect, shining like topaz only in springtime.

The man would take refuge at the Fiumecaldo, among the horsetails and the crabs, when he longed for his daughter, for the living breath of her, for the blessed sight of her. We were told that down there he read the Upanishads and the precepts of Shivaism, where it is said that non-being must not be meditated upon because it lacks all sentience. He had received those texts as a gift from Father Onorio the Capuchin in return for various aromatic plants that grow on mountain summits. There Dolcissimo met the goatherds who came up from the lowlands along the slopes of the Erei. Up there the ruminants could feed peacefully on wild chicory, grain, and sheepgrass. The goatherds were already few, very old, deaf, disturbed by the luminous springs that rose from stony globes and mantles of dried plants. If they were not sleeping or gazing ecstatically at the boundless countryside, during the afternoon counterhours, they would be whittling walking sticks while they watched the exhalations from pockets of mercury and sardonyx.

I told Mario Sinus that in the past Zebulonia had about seven thousand sheep and as many goats, every inhabitant having one milker. The sheep were medium size, with pointed ears capable of perceiving the hiss of the snakes and the weaving and unweaving of the spiders. Males and females looked the same, both had horns and a thin tuft of wool at the chin. Most of the goats were a domestic species of *hircus,* and the sheep were Barbary, though up in the mountains you found the wild *hircus,* hairy and so sensitive it could feel the librations of the moon. The goats weighed an average of forty kilograms; the Barbary sheep had strength, soft pelts, and a great resistance to the canicular heat.

We know, brother Timor, that goat's milk, contrary to common belief, is nourishing and sweet, easy to digest, filling the labyrinths of the tongue with sweetness to heighten the perceptions of our senses. A mixture of goat and sheep milk was used to make ricotta in sheepfolds or in caves shaded by carob trees, and a variety of other kinds of cheese. The very soft one called *tuma;* the *first-salt,* to be eaten at sunrise; the wide variety of fermented ones, and lastly the peppered one we call *piacentino,* which grated over pasta and oil dispels melancholy and makes us love our own body.

Every peasant kept some wheels of these cheeses in baskets covered with wet cloths, or under the

bed on a layer of straw. A great quantity was sold
in towns and villages throughout the island all the
way to Akragas.* Often the donkeys that
transported crates of cheese were entrusted to boys,
who amused themselves calling to each other, their
echoes crossing groves, precipices, and vineyards.
It was not uncommon to find cheeses fallen from
sacks and crates under the thousandfruitbearing
hackberry, which we called *millicucchi,* or in the
crevices of the Coste or along the banks of the
brooks. The crows caught sight of them from high
up and came down in flocks to peck at them.

I told Sinus that the goatherds called their
animals by name, so that passing along through the
countryside, it was not uncommon to hear:
"Riricchia, where are you? Prosapia, come here!
Get back here, Sognante! Yaquinedda, where do
you think you are going? Ftonia, what are you
scared of? Giocasta, where've you gone?"

The herdsmen did not kill their sheep, knowing
that the images emanating from the animals brought
health and salvation, but the butchers, my grandfather Don Papè among them, sold the meat that
had been spiced with fennel and pistachio and
dried the skins at Fuoriporta. Out of them cradles
and jackets were made, and out of the wool shawls
and lace trim for dresses.

But the true craft of stitchery had been learned
by our women from the sisters of the orphanage
who came from Andalusia and Catalonia. Linen,
canvas, cretonne, muslin, and damask were brought
to Zebulonia by small merchants who came back to
pick them up when the needlework was done. The
women of Zebulonia, sitting in their doorways to
take advantage of the shafts of sunlight or the noc-

turnal starlight, worked with embroidery hoops, frames, spindles, and spools. (All things that became obsolete with technological progress.) In silence mothers and daughters did the open-work stitch, the Paris-stitch, the shadow-stitch, but they were particularly famous for their pulled-thread work. To embroider those fabrics they used silk, guipure, spools of the thinnest silver thread, and, to achieve a special lustre, thread infused with gold dust.

Since the people of the town had always been poor, grains their main food, and the children and old people longed wildly to see non-existent worlds, the women let themselves go on that byssus and muslin, trying to reproduce great rivers in leafy shade, lunar births, pansies, pitchers overflowing with the Lord's tears, fantastic nectar dripping from blue tree trunks, cornucopias spilling green coins.

Yaluna, as we saw, had even embroidered paradise on a bed cover. On feast days all those quilted spreads, capes, tablecloths – before the merchants came to collect them, paying for them mostly in foodstuffs – were displayed on balconies, window grilles, and rooftops. When the girls from the orphanage were summoned to take part in funeral processions, they wore sumptuous black shawls on which dark trees, ruined castles, and dying comets were embroidered.

Dolcissimo helped to bring back the art of the needle when Zebulonia was in decline and the silk vendors, the buyers of hair, and the merchants disappeared. Michelangelo Buglio had introduced the agave in the region and also, after living among Arab pirates for a time, the palm tree. These trees were not appreciated by the peasants because the agave never produced anything except its tall straight flowers, and the palm never brought its bunches of dates to maturity. In the fertile blackness of the soil, they spread by spontaneous reproduction. From the trunk of the agave and the fans of the palm Dolcissimo extracted threads that, dried, could be used in place of the spools of cotton thread. Eventually the women of Zebulonia were reduced to making clothes out of them to protect themselves from the raw heat of summer steaming from the stones. Buglio had also succeeded in bringing to Zebulonia some exotic birds, soon destroyed by the arrogance of the Spanish rulers who hunted them to eat their meat with the Jesuits. They sent the plumage all the way to Madrid where the rulers had ornaments made for the hats and veils of their women. A few birds of paradise, purple parrots, sacred ibis, and lyre birds escaped the slaughter. Dolcissimo searched for them in the intricate valley of the Trezzito, where 'Alqama, who loved the mobility of the sky and the creatures that fly in it, could spot them among the oaks and the olive trees. A lyre bird and a bird of paradise that were caught were brought to Zebulonia for the pleasure of the children, who came from every section of town to admire them.

When 'Alqama's mind snapped, her father wandered through the valleys to see the rising cloud formations. They reminded him of his daughter whose mind was spinning with the earth. Thus he learned that spiral clouds rose from ravines, cumulus from wild, impassible, foggy fields, and that cirrus clouds formed when the sun suddenly dried the film of air on the trunks of trees.

All this, according to Sinus, increased the emotional imbalance of Dolcissimo himself, leading him to dwell on the inner world and the vanity of exterior things.

Yaluna said that the man was driven by the memory of his daughter to follow the sunsets. "You know," she said, "when I went to look for chicory, I would see Dolcissimo and 'Alqama running after the sun setting behind the mountains. He would tell his daughter: 'You'll see that we'll catch up with it. It follows the course of the Fiumecaldo, where the axis of the world is, and we'll see it from below getting larger and larger. Come on, run!' Left alone by his daughter's illness, he followed the setting sun through ferns and brambles."

And you know, brother Timor, that sunsets are very long in our region, due to the vast solar refractions that rise in the deserts and are reflected by the depths of the sea.

Dolcissimo would weep, surrounded by the multitude of yellow points the sunset kindled from the live mercury and copper dust encased in the solid rock. As evening fell, he would weep over the dead snakes, the fields, and the well of Timucah. Meanwhile the light from the immense spaces of the west was deserting the stones and the amethyst crystals.

At this point Mario Sinus said, "Ariete, this land of vast sunsets nurtures men who cultivate the earth, women who long for water sources, and Capricorn horses capable of thought."

V

A central point of our inquiry concerned the departure of my mother Algazèlia, who with a small group of Zebulonians had gone in search of water. This, in my town, had always been scarce, although sweet and soft, both the spring flowing into the Quattro Canali and the upper one of the Sei Canali, and lastly the aquifer of Salònia, which originated in the vicinity of Burchiaturo. This had been cunningly seized, with the legal assistance of the regional government, by Baron B. of Burchiaturo to irrigate his immense fields of artichokes, celery, spikenard, sweet lemons, and cinnamon trees. I had become involved in the problem when I was health officer there, but I never got anywhere except for a reprimand I received from the regional commissioner of agriculture.*

The channel of the Quattro Canali aquifer, opened with celebrations and great ringing of bells at the end of the last century, flowed close to the surface in the thickets of the Impiccato valley, where it was discovered by the wild goats that gathered there toward evening together with the thirsty crows, lost herds of oxen, and the sacred scarabs that infested the surrounding mountains.

The spring of the Sei Canali disappeared suddenly when an earthquake opened a chasm under the craggy slope of the Pietre Nere. The children, left to themselves by the departure of their emigrant parents, gathered there to hear, their ears to the ground, a sucking and hissing of waves cascading in the bowels of the region.

The lack of drinking water caused an uprising of women and old men, but the local authorities, in collusion with the corrupt ruling party, did nothing. Unused for years, the ruined cisterns held black, polluted water. Yaluna said that the boiling heat of summer made the poor Zebulonians dream forever of fountains and brooks singing in whirlpools of silence. Most people adapted to the biweekly allotments of water, and on the other days resorted to juicy fruits like watermelons, to the clear liquid that filtered through north-facing walls, to the occasional light autumn rains, and to their own tears. In others that hardship increased the disorders of old age, and the emotions that spill over into anxiety. That is, Sinus explained, the customary rhythm of their inner time was upset: in the absence of the sense of the future that makes room for physical spatialization, the present condensed upon itself as it had with 'Alqama. The past did not illuminate it by pushing it along in the common vital current. And in the absence of the future, all those people lost their feeling for the infinite space around, they no longer believed either in their children, or in the fragrant flowers of the lavatic soil.

My mother, left without any of her five children, became a pole of attraction for the other discontented people. She made an agreement with Tèlefo, who earned a living as a swordswallower in the nearby towns, and with the sorcerer Abrucàl, one of those magicians who in Zebulonia invoked the rain, or killed the worms in babies by abdominal friction and chants learned at midnight on December 31, when, as the stars multiply, the land prepares for

the flowering of the almond trees. They were
joined by Mnémio, the blind man, and his guides,
an old goat and his young niece Yacomina, an
orphan since birth. The strangest characters in that
group were my Uncle Michele and Ops. The
former, who had married my mother's sister Pipí (I
lived with them a long time since they had no
children), as a young man had abandoned his trade
as a shoemaker and emigrated to New York, where
he and his wife worked in a shirt factory, as my
mother did a short time later. He used to read the
fragments of Democritus and Empedocles and
through them attempted to explain the universe,
which he believed to be made of islands of stars
animated by a fertile male force, and by a female
one that sowed disorder. He was reading me *The
Wonders of the Heavens* by Camille Flammarion
when unexpectedly, by some strange coincidence,
the comet of Father Onorio rose in the sky. With
its long tail and white arms it brought us white
eggs and streams over the roofs, from which we
children collected the light in buckets and tubs for
the nights of darkness to come. On that occasion,
the old women, sitting among the saplings growing
from the eaves, or on their balconies, contrary to
their customary modesty, relieved themselves in the
chamber pots called cànteri.*

My uncle's passions were roses and goldfinches.
He cultivated the former on his farm at Nunziata,
at the foot of Mt. Carratabbía (where recently
graffiti of small elephants of the mesozoic era were
discovered in a cave). He had some splendid ones,
many-petaled, starshaped, purple, but his pride was
the hybrid rose that, imitating the grafting skills of
his townsmen, he had succeeded in obtaining after

years of effort: it was ephemeral, that is, it bloomed and died in one day; but as the seeds were fertilized, new roses bloomed continuously from the dry shoots, with different colors on the same petals, as in the beautiful-by-night. He had come back from America with about fifty cages of goldfinches, which he arranged on his three balconies just below the Church of St. Francis, which reverberates in storms. Their nests and their chirping attracted the poor children from all parts of town. When I was six we used to go and get the fledgling sparrows under the rooftiles of the houses of Mario Privitera and Canon Símili to fill the cages that we made at the Nunziata farm. The mother sparrows detected their own little ones on the balcony of that country house and came with great fluttering of wings and beaks to feed them vetch and other seeds.

Once my Uncle Michele bought from Dolcissimo a lyrebird that sang from morning to night to the glory of God, but very soon it grew sad, accustomed as it was to the summer cool of the woods of the Trezzito. They called it Lu. It died. My uncle had it stuffed so that the peasants could see the display of its feathers. He took it along when he went with the others to look for wells and streams.

Among the people most sensitive to the lack of water were the few remaining poets. My town has a long tradition that seems to go back to the Siculi whose funereal dirges and hostile taunting of the July sun that scorches the countryside are still remembered.

Of these there remains some uncertain evidence on the tombs cut into Mt. Carratabbía mentioned above, among bushes, myrtle, and huge wild fennel: graffiti outlined in tiny dots of red kermes and with an ochre wash, representing men following a corpse stretched out on poles. In another children gesticulate angrily at a large sphere above them burning trees with its powerful rays.

There is no trace in Zebulonia of the Siculian comedy of Epicharmos, while contradictory sources would have us believe that Stesichoros' penchant for mythmaking survives, just as Theocritus' elegy could be heard as late as thirty years ago in the rhythms of crotals, sistra, and pipes brought to Sicily from Asia Minor. A certain moralizing mimiambic taste combined a pleasing country grace with mordant accents that were a kind of synthesis of the Etruscan *fescennini* and the Roman *satyra*. Of the Arab poets Ibn Hamdis who died in Seville in 1121, Alì Ibn Katà who made an anthology of Sicilian Arabic poets, and the mathematician and geographer Erdrisi who constructed armillary spheres and silver planispheres, there is an indirect memory in those Zebulonians who take up their motifs in passionate melancholy when they are far from their own country, or when, walking alone through the desolate feudal estates, they ask the god of the poor to make the land bloom again.

But the poet dearest to my townspeople is Paolo Maura, whose jail poems, aphorisms, and witticisms are still repeated, and whose poem *La Pigghiata,* on his arrest for motives of love, ending in the dark Vicaria Prison in Palermo, is sought by those who can get it in manuscript form. On the anniversary of the death of Maura, which occurred on September 24, 1711, at the fair that takes place on the Lavatoio Road under the eucalyptus trees, the poets of Zebulonia hold competitions, taking as their subject the universals of the earth, the rustling of trees, the tunes of the last cicadas, the circling of the bumble bees above the caper flowers. We have lost the custom of going to Timucah, where, among thousands of stones with clinging fossil shells, there is a boulder that used to inspire the poets gathered there from all the provinces of Sicily. It has been established that in those geological strata earthquakes break through; the round utricles of any vegetable or animal or ornithological seed experience violent growth; and the gravitational curves of the earth, and those that swing as they fall from the sky, come together and give plenitude to those who perceive them.

Even my father, a tailor in his youth, secretly wrote poems that I collected under the title *L'Arcano* (Frosinone: Bianchini, 1975), but did not participate in the dithyrambic competitions held in Zebulonia, extemporaneous poetic games that expressed bitterness, political ridicule, joy in the pleasures of the autumn season, and marvelous conceits on oats, barley, and the mysterious fruit luldaghelí. Unfortunately the custom subsided with the coming of fascism.*

The last of the Zebulonian rhapsodists learned about the adventure of my mother Algazèlia; they celebrated her with the help of primitive painters whose large pictures were divided into small squares, vivid with brilliant vegetable dyes and ochre powder. These singers had been particularly struck by the disappearance of Ops, who, together with Don Filippo Fichera, was considered the best poet, once Massaro Turi Alía, Carcò, and Sframeli had died.

Ops also played the violin. He had made one for himself using the old wooden back of a similar instrument left by a friar in our grandfather's shop. He had made the strings out of lamb's intestines, the bladders of brook fish, and agave fibers braided with the plumage of a hawk.

"Oh, come," Yaluna called at about noon, which in that September arrived in long solar vapors from the gentled peaks and from the purple flowers of the chicory.

"Oh, where?" I asked.

"Don't you know that they have made motets on the disappearance of Ops, Don Michele, and mother Algazèlia?"

The small Piazza dei Vespri, which through the house of my paternal grandfather opens into Piazza Buglio, already bright with luminous shafts, was full of the old men of Zebulonia in their black caps.

A rhapsodist ("It's Amarú," Yaluna said), with the boy Mercurio beside him tuning the sadness of his silver clarinet to the poetic discourse, was recounting the supposed fate of the group that had gone in search of water. Interested in these sorts of performances, and even fond of them, Sinus recorded the song that the wonderfully eloquent sound of the clarinet carried along the balconies and roofs.

I set it down here.

DEPARTURE

Alas, alas! grieving we depart, doubting our
    hope
and our desire, with neither oar nor sail,
led by the glitter of lava,
uranium, and drooping asphodels!

Master masons, stone cutters, dyers in purple,
carry wrapped in shining cloaks
and sweet ambrosia infants
already dead in the sun's fires.

In our likeness the women follow,
gatherers of rue, and the blind poet Mnémio,
Ops with his violin, and Lu, the mounted bird,
Tèlefo, the great swordswallower,
and, trailed by the Dwarf with his horn,
the sorcerer Abrucàl in shining chastity
tells the high risen echo that the lost
'Alqama is our noble lady.

In the remains of a day dying vermilion,
we depart in procession from our homes,
betrayed by our mountain,
abandoned, their lamps snuffed out,
invaded by pale grasses where
a griffon in aging plumage is gripped
in the sickness unto death, which in wonder
we see in the eyes of the struggling bird.

No gushing of springs we found here,
only dark cisterns,
vain images of distracted minds,
their mournful lamentation fearful
returning to our trembling ears
Ops' violin. Out of them issued,
shivering, mad with fright,
the dark children of the cliff.

So we move through narrow lanes
circling craters where the excessive day
is at its peak. O death – cheat, betrayer,

you left us in so short a time
and in this wave of daylight
bring to our heart a thirst for water,
that bears to mortal plants delight, and to the
    God
a welcome place among peacock feathers.

Our mother Algazèlia, feeling within her
the sparkling of water, and precious stone,
like a jay repeating its shrill call
in simple clarity, speaks:
"Wretched in the deep sources
of our fear, why do we wait
to leave these deadly bolts of heat
for the deep springs, in the ruin of July?"

The gusts of the easterlies burned
in the depths of the skies. And the sweet waning
of days over the curved moonless gardens,
and the vanishing of rivers, and our anger
at the lost grains and fava beans,
gently guided us,
men deprived of thought,
and behind us, women in a brightening of rays.

As we walk in that flaring of heat,
our wise Algazèlia, our lily, our rose,
shows us a spring, a starved thread
under colored limestone, forgotten place now a
    haven
for black-feathered crows, all flutter and
    bobbing.
The old in the darts of the sun
throw their seeds in their hunger,
with the luminous sweep of the sower.

The crows swoop to the safety
of the blazing olive groves; and the Dwarf
blows his horn in resounding wide circles
to call back the doves, the Sagittarian horses,
and the scattered bones. Tèlefo
spins hot winds and wandering mesons
into rubies and blades of flowers
over shimmering water, a dying salamander.

Lacking an empty but beckoning future,
those Zebulonians curl up in their past,
the golden spring has changed to a sphinx!
To lighten the sadness of leaving,
Algazèlia, our bird and our beacon, reveals
that the splendid heart shape of the fava
and the kernel that swells in the earth like a
    moon,
in their windy chambers enclose our God.

Algazèlia thus ends her beginning:
"Brothers, divine links in the chain, if June
lords it up there in lightning,
hot gusts, blazes of sun over wheatfields,
below in the night of the earth there are eggs
to feed with albumen and honey the hands
of the old who are marked out by death
and the children unraveling the numbers of
    mortals."

Then the wisdom of Uncle Michele
leads them into the land of Timucah,
rich in wells, loved by bees, laced in copper
and itterbion. As night falls on the crew,
they lie under echoes of olive groves.
Adorned there by crickets and the whistling air

of the peaks, they pulse in a shimmer of darkness
with the flickering intelligence of trees.

The old in their sleep, forgetting their sons,
wind among sweet sounds of caves and of woods
    and of mountains,
through the waves of blue rivers
under the Bear, in advance of the light.
Before dawn opens the orient sky
into cool lunar gardens
and a gathering of shimmering lights
the people conversing continue their journey.

Up there, in a narrowing of paths
and a gleaming of peaks sadness dissolves,
in the gold of the earth the reluctance
of the limbs. In the vermilion of stones
and the gleam of their needles
the travelers are radiant. Out of the plaintive
and glorious well of the stars,
the earth rises.

No more than two hours on their way
(we are saddened now mourning the loss of
    them),
they see among branches and sweet scent of
    water,
in the highland, their well.
As the day sweeps by in a friendship of winds,
they see herdsmen and goats,
still, in a shimmering and flaming of stones
and women among sapphires, lovely, shielding
    their eyes.

In praise of July cicadas and ants
bring sweetness beyond measure of songs and
    guitars
to the figtree and the robin that circles
from the well to the sky; the perfumes
are flowing downvalley toward our people
where a pomegranate wheels
in the play of its light
among bees and the last stalks of beans.

Assailed by dark thirst,
our people lean over the wall of the well,
dappled by mosses and light from the east;
deep draughts of water, and in the bucket
a few red snails: a sight of great joy.
From under a rosy-mouthed figtree
Algazèlia directs that the women
give thanks for the well.

Ops on his violin, the Dwarf on his horn,
and the women in the longing of their eyes,
remembering laughter and joy,
dispel their dark worries. The spring,
in dark remote tremors, wells up
rustling under the star of the Ram.
For two days they cluster like birds
by the well's dazzling clarity.

The freedom of kings and of lords is their own
    now.
Having with hawthorn and incense
gained lordship of time, a fiery space,
Algazèlia, our lily of the valley, in longing
for Fiumecaldo's waters returns to
the journey, with sparks in her eyes,

and leaves in her hair, and the splendor
of Aries clasped again in her hands.

The ebbing waters of the stream summon
our people where the robin twitters
and the chatter of pistachios swells the young
    shoots
in the crevices, sown (night had come)
by the sparkling of far strings of stars.
Then daylight returns, and noontime; in the
    afternoon
counterhours shifting the breeze from the valley
comes riding, on honey and dazzling horses.

As evening extends over almonds and hedges
of boisterous blackbirds, and eddies in the
    Fiumecaldo,
Algazèlia loses her wisdom and flowers,
and takes pleasure in hawks, in abandon to time;
in their hands in the water the women now
    nourish
a feeling for death, and their men on the
    opposite bank
are observing the mortal procession
in the dim upper air under fiery Mercury.

Over the water Uncle Michele joins the voices
of death that call to a gathering pollens and
    gnats
and wandering swords. From the bed of the
    stream
copper and mercury are drawn and transfixed
    into trees.
Abrucàl, the sorcerer, and Tèlefo
in ochre in the caves of the mountains paint

the ox with its plow,
the goats and the whirlwind.

The women are praying for Chastity and Poverty,
like a moon that is doubled in topaz
and, as music, in the branches of almond trees.
The dead children are laid on the stones
of the river in fullness of light.
Algazèlia, the mistress of peaks, as the day
dies like a unicorn, tells them to search
for the first water that has no wave.

And the group moves again
like high shafts of light through the woods.
Around them no chancing of sparrows,
but sky without end. Through branches
of myrrh and clear distances
our people are watching the sunset resplendent
on lodestones and oaktrees. The women
sway among rocks in the wind of the evening.

All are thinking of time long past,
a maddened peacock lacking a center,
youth broken, expanding its fan
in spiraling flights.
It is ruin for our people
and for her, Algazèlia, our lady most gentle.
When Capricorn raises its stars,
the owl hoots to the black basilisks of time.

When daylight returns in the pleasure of leaves,
they catch sight of the source
of the stream Fiumecaldo, that gathers through
    rocks,
dripping through thickets of fennel and fern.

Uncle Michele counts twenty such grottoes
under the rustling heights.
Eyes wide among myrtles they kneel at the
    source,
reflecting the last of the horns of the moon.

Humbly they nourish themselves until night
at the vein that rises in rumbles of silence
in spurts and sighs of love
from mantles of dripping and splashing
among topaz, and lichens, and pale rounded
    stones.
Mnémio, the blind man, scenting the fragrance
    of horsetail,
discovers Dolcissimo
asleep by the watery murmuring banks.

A longing in some of them springs up
for sea breezes blowing as one
over rock salt and fugitive channels.
But the old folk and sweet Algazèlia,
greeting Dolcissimo, say
that the harp of the sea and the voice of the
    dolphin,
lost in the high winds of moondrawn tides,
without hope, without goats, were not in their
    stars.

At this point the Zebulonian rhapsodist fell
silent with his finger on the last picture, where
mountains and valleys were distinct in the
foreground and the blue sea in the distance.
    "Did you like the song?" Yaluna asked us. "In
Zebulonia, as you can see, everything is trans-
formed in the mouths of these philosophers."

The singer had turned the painted poster and, making the boy Mercurio take up the ringing flame of his clarinet again, directed his voice to the many small squares in which, half-hidden among arboreal details, a little god was glimpsed, intertwined with roots and clumps of earth.

"The god of the poor!" exclaimed the audience, baring their heads in respect, while the storyteller continued and ended his song to Mercurio's Argus-eyed music.

Beside us Yaluna bowed her head respectfully and the voice of the rhapsodist rose:

Vainly your reverence for water is
burning your senses, in you
the horn and the violin turn to
a purple embroidery of numbers.

In a regal robe of agreement,
from your dreams,
the spirit is first born, and the light
of the waves in which man is bathed.

Every spring holds enigmas, thoughts,
the wonder of what has been born,
era, time, idea,
birds, nourishment, lymph.

Where no spring is, no truth,
you are drowned in the heart of the night,
old ones, our saviors, you walk
with the nymphs in perfection of light.

Dolcissimo

And metals, and crystals, and olive trees,
come under your rule,
and the Ram in the sky:
constellations take fire in your soul!

VI

On Mario Sinus' insistence, we directed our investigation to the cemetery, which sheltered all who had died in the last hundred years.

"Oh, leave the dead to their fate," Yaluna complained when she heard about it. Though unwilling, she followed us, useful because she could tell us so much about the families that were gone.

"Ariete, I'm doing this for your sake!" she sighed.

We went through Fuoriporta along the wide road that looked out in a great circle to the hills and valleys. We went through Ràbbato.

"What's this?" asked the psychiatrist when he saw the small abandoned village. Heaps of straw green with mold surrounded the tiny houses.

"Ràbbato," I told my friend, "seems to come from the Arab word *rabà*, which means a blend, a mixture of pigments. Its inhabitants, who handed down the craft from father to son, made pitchers with special clays."

"Taùggyi, little pitchers," Yaluna added. "What variety! They made dishes, jars, heads of saints, rooftiles, piggybanks, and funeral masks for the rich."

In fact they even stamped inscriptions taken from the Bible or the Koran or the Upanishads into the clay. They also made incense burners sheathed in bronze, lustre goblets, fake coins glazed with copper oxide that were given to the children, who played with them, tossing handfuls of them in the streets, among the trees, against the sun.

Walking and talking we arrived, through a steep, narrow lane, at the cemetery gate. On the left was the monastery of the Capuchins, built in the sixteenth century, now in a state of decay. It had been a residence for Friars Minor, who had by now dwindled to three old men. "Why don't we go in?" Yaluna asked, pulling a thin cord that rang a little bell.

"O Father Onorio," she shouted, "do open, Father Onorio!"

"What do you want?" said Father Onorio, opening. He was a short man, with a very white face

"This is Ariete. Don't you remember him? He's the son of Don Nanè the tailor. He'd like to visit the monastery with his friend."

He looked at us doubtfully. His eyes had no lashes.

"Come in! What do you expect to find here?"

We entered a courtyard with a well in the middle.

"It has the freshest water," Yaluna said.

In faded paint on the walls you could make out fake columns, with simulated capitals, and just above them, little windows, at each of which stood a pot of sunflowers and a pot of red peppers.

"The sunflowers," Friar Onorio explained, noting our curiosity, "tell us with the shifting of their shadows how the sun rises and travels through the valleys. They indicate the time for our lamentations and speak to us of the passing of life. The pepper we rub on our bread for supper. There's only three of us left now, Father Bonaventura, Father Stellario and myself."

On the left side of the courtyard there was a kitchen garden, a tangle of weeds. In a low voice I told Sinus that as boys we used to come to the monastery for confession. Ten, twenty of us. We knew that in that garden grew the laughing herb, a hybrid of the hundred-eyed euphrasia, the radiant *stellina,* and a wrinkled, thornless cactacea. To ward off the fear of the dead who might follow us from the nearby cemetery carrying jugs full of tears on their shoulders, we tore off sprigs of that herb and chewed on them – it made us see double, put thunder in our ears, cheerfulness in our hands, and breath in our lungs.

"Do you still have the laughing herb?" Yaluna asked. "We used to come to get leaves of it to mix with the grass for the goats and the bran for the roosters. The goats – can you imagine? – made so much milk, and the roosters sang through the whole town till midnight."

"Who knows, Yaluna," the monk answered, "whether it still grows in that garden? Let's take the doctor upstairs."

Going up a well-worn staircase, we found ourselves in a corridor where there was a clock in a case with the inscription *"tempus fugit irreparabile."*

"Here are our books," said Father Onorio, opening a door into a dark room.

A good number of books were ranged on shelves, but we saw many piled on chairs and in corners.

"There are about thirty thousand," our escort explained. "Beyond that door there are two more rooms full of them. Since 1548 our brothers have left the symbol of the eye in every book, and their thirst for knowledge."

He showed us a Latin-Spanish-Sicilian dictionary that helped the monks, who came from the most distant regions of the world, to communicate with each other. We saw books by the Fathers of the Church, theological tracts by Father Nìgido of Mineo, the encyclopedia of D'Avino, works by Segneri, Rosmini, the Christological series edited by Migne, Cantù's work, Redi's book on the generation of insects, Ptolemy's *Tetrabiblon,* the Teubner edition of the *Astronomica* of Marcus Manilius. We opened some and between the pages found sprigs of sanguinaria, catnip, sprays of celandine, all probably used as fragrant bookmarks to help one forget the sense of the ephemeral.

Ancient Father Onorio showed us the Picatrix manuscript of the great Arab magician Albumasar that the Spanish king Alphonsus had had translated from Arabic into Spanish in 1256. Here men were invited to consider the stars as motive forces of life, and there was reference to the ideal city similar to the al-Asmunain of Trimegistus. On a bookstand we saw a huge sheepskin Koran in kufic characters, the red scalloped fastenings of its cover depicting angels in prayer with blue wings opened to the orient.

"Oh, yes," smiled the monk, "we've had a great deal of traffic with mankind. For us men, animals, and stones are all brothers."

On the page to which the book lay open we read the sura of the cave: "The parable of earthly life is like water that we cause to fall from the sky, and which mixes with the earth's vegetation; the next day, however, it becomes stubble that the winds disperse." The verses bearing the number 30 read: "Those who believe in the fire of the stars and in

87

the imponderable shall possess the gardens of Eden beneath which the rivers run; in them (in the rivers), they shall be adorned with golden bracelets and wear green garments of silk and brocade; they shall recline on raised couches."

We left. In the bare cells, where you could feel the reverberation of the pepper plants, we found Father Stellario contemplating a salamander sleeping at the bottom of a bowl, and Father Bonaventura who wore a little sardonyx snake on his left wrist. He recognized me.

"Oh, Ariete!" he said. "Have you come back to us?"

Since it was the hour for prayer, we left them in the church, a small temple with a wooden trapdoor of sycamore at its center, brought there by Phrygian eremites. It must certainly have led to an underground chamber. There was no main altar, only sandstone benches with armrests of black zeolite.

"Goodbye," said the old men, beginning to sing their psalms, suras from the Koran, mixed with logia, Orphic hymns, and sayings from the Upanishads. From some goatskin bags arranged along the arches, cleverly manipulated, came the lamentations of the *invisivel realidade*. Once outside, we entered the cemetery through the half-open gate, descending the concrete steps. In an open space on the left, where at that moment the reddish light of early afternoon prevailed, we saw the marble bust of Luigi Capuana,* covered with climbing wild roses that grew from the mouth of two old artillery shells. Below that open space, the cemetery stretched out before us in two rectangular wings of terraced land. Surrounding it were barren fields and ravines.

"Do you see how much light there is?" Yaluna told us. "We've improved it with the money the emigrants send from Switzerland."

There were pale blue tombstones, crude plaster statues of the dead, angels, lighted votive lamps, and copper scaffolding supporting the crumbling earth.

I understood what you have told me, brother Timor: in life we are encased by time in cellular glomeruli where nothingness takes shape, while in the cemeterial space we are all close together as we once were.

Yaluna began pointing out the dead: Baron Spadaro, an old man with long sideburns, who died at the end of the last century; Pino Símili, smiling from the photograph in its niche; Aunt Aitedda and Uncle Antonio Casaccio, her husband, whose faces lived again through the brilliant clarity of the air; my paternal grandparents, who still in the fullness of life looked out toward the last glimmers of summer; and Massaro Filippo Mammana, with whom as a boy I played cards in the Nunziata countryside where I spent several months of each year with my Uncle Michele and my Aunt Pipí: during the hottest hours of the afternoon, under the grape arbor, I would read to old Massaro Filippo the fragments of Democritus that belonged to my Uncle Michele, and he would say yes, it was quite possible that the sun and the moon had torn themselves away in a vortex from the Milky Way. In a corner we saw Pino Scatà, who looked at us benevolently from the slab of gray marble under which he was buried.

I heard myself called: "Oh, doctor, doctor."

89

It was Margarone, the cemetery custodian. We embraced in remembrance of our seven years of solidarity when I was Public Health Officer.

"How glad I am to see you again," he said. "Yaluna is with you, too? Have you seen how much we've improved this cemetery? Now it's easy to find the dead and talk to them."

From the wild olives of the chapel of the master craftsmen some blackbirds flew off whistling. We entered. All the departed artisans of Zebulonia were buried there. I saw my Uncle Michele, who was smiling at me, and stopped a long time to look at him ("Oh, Ariete!" I thought I heard him call). Below, in the sarcophagus that was reached through a funnel staircase, was my Aunt Pipí, my mother's sister. Blond, with bluish ash in her eyes, she seemed at ease in the endless voyage of death.

"O Ariete!" she called. "Are you here? My heart is pounding, my child, you whom I nourished with milk and morsels of bread in the evil days of your fever. Do you remember the comet that used to come over our house? Are you still eager to discover the mystery of God?"

Oh, did I answer yes?

"I cannot get out of here, nor can you enter. But my mind is clear. Do you remember that you wanted to fly with the wings of our rooster? Uncle Michele cut them, skillfully, dotting them with red, like rubies, and attached them to you, and you flew for a bit over the figs and mulberry trees of the Nunziata?"

"Why can't I enter, Aunt Pipí?"

"How can you, you who can still see, hear, smell?"

From the top of the stairs Yaluna called: "Ariete, is your Aunt Pipí talking to you? If you knew how good she was at baking bread! Your grandfather Turi couldn't do without her."

Because of the small size of the chapel many craftsmen were buried outside, along the walls. Because their lives had been dedicated to the harmony of blocks of stone, of clothing, pitchers, and planed walnut, their relatives, in the fragrant earth around the graves, had planted the sweet lemon, the bloodorange, the tangeorange, and the tangerine that has bluish fruits.

"Oh, doctor, are you daydreaming down there?" the custodian Margarone called.

"In certain stretches of our journey," my aunt Pipí concluded, "we on this side enjoy coolness and gaiety. Water, sometimes dark, springs from our arms; there are no olive trees, no lizards, but we can drink at all the rivers. Ariete, has your seed sprouted, on that side? Are you happy, my son?"

I did not answer. With Mario Sinus we went to visit my father, who lies in the chapel of my Uncle Turi Casaccio: my grandfather and my grandmother Casaccio and Uncle Turi are in the upper section; and in the lower right section is my father. In these years, you, my brother Timor, have come every day to pound with your fist on our father's vault. At first you heard a dull noise because there was a body inside, a whole body, still earth and water. Gradually, as it decomposed (the hands, the thoughts, the ears) the sound became hollow, and hollowness is an emptiness quantifiable in nothingness.

"What peace! Do you feel it?" Yaluna asked.

Silence issued from the young cypresses and, deepening over the graves, gathered over my father's vault.

"You should see," Margarone added a little later, "at night from this point Saturn can be seen, rippling its light against the blackness."

"The silence, in slow circles," Sinus interjected, "must penetrate your father's bones."

"Oh, don't you want to see them?" Yaluna said. "Stunted twigs they are now, those confines in which his soul must pace! And you, Margarone, when the ripples of Saturn's light come, don't you feel Don Nanè looking for the blaze of his children in his own bones?"

"She's raving," Margarone whispered to me. "She's over eighty. Don't mind her. Unfortunately the problem of the common grave remains as it was when you were here, doctor."

He showed it to us at the edge of the levelled ground of the cemetery. It was a hole in the ground that expanded into a grotto, containing shin bones, shoulder blades, skulls with black hair. Since the wind of March bears pollen, some of it had fallen there. Among those remains grew an orange tree, a twisted sycamore, the hollow trunk of a sterile carob, their tiny roots clinging to the bones.

"No, don't look!" the custodian Margarone exclaimed. "Come, I'll show you a strange place that I've been able to locate by means of special calculations."

It was at the end of the main path. Following the directions of the custodian, we realized that the gaze of the eyes of the pictures of the dead and of the little terracotta angels flowed, as if along luminous threads, straight into our eyes, in a single perspective.

"If I feel low," Margarone concluded, "I sit on this rock," he pointed to it, "to take in at a glance the feelings and the fears of the dead. Who better than I, believe me, far from the living as I am?"

VII

After our visit to the Capuchins Mario Sinus grew restless and often fell into gloomy moods unusual for him. I tried to divert him by engaging him in the study of the speech of the Zebulonians, which appeared reclusive and constricting to him; capable of the lively flow of narrative only when it dealt with the past. In his notes, which I found later, he said that it was a speech lacking exuberance, little suited to dialog, although permeated by a singsong gentleness. So much so that it lent itself to phonic subdivisions that almost rhymed. Sinus maintained that it was a tactile language, with its open and palatalized final vowels and its many internal diphthongations. It vibrated in one's hands, succeeding through reverberations of sound in establishing the sensory world in one's body cavities. It expressed doubts, perspicuity, and melancholy. In the women it became an olfactory speech because the words not only transmitted the flashing of the heart, they captured from the external world the fragrance of herbs and burning rocks.

To define the qualities of Zebulonian speech, Sinus begged Yaluna to take us into courtyards, back alleys, parts of the town we had not seen.

"This way, this way," the little old woman would say.

Many streets were totally uninhabited. There were many chickens that had reproduced on their own, hatching in mangers, in haylofts, under the

saplings on the roofs. Eggs could be found everywhere: in holes, on the ground among the parietaria,
in clay washed down by the rain, or at the head of
paths that led into the countryside. They were a
dazzling white, with a tinge of purple. So Sinus
would smile and say: "They give more color to
Zebulonia in the early morning when the light is
most brilliant."

Since no egg traders were coming from the
nearby towns anymore, the children played with
those eggs, rolling them down the slopes, or
drawing the eyes of their far-away mothers on them.

The goats too, left to themselves, had
multiplied, and you saw many of them, browsing on
dry grass among the stones. Some old woman
would suckle their teats to satisfy her hunger and
then milk out the udders so the animal would not
suffer. Thus it happened that we saw milk flowing
down from all the knolls of the town that morning,
down through gutters and ditches, around the trunks
of wild fig trees that grew in the streets. Being of
different sorts, one type of milk evaporated from
the stones, another would coagulate, producing soft
ricotta; where the ground had an even temperature
and did not break the little waves of milk as they
flowed from higher ground, the milky substance did
not thicken at all, but retained its liquid
transparency. The children who ran to drink that
milk would even tell us, with their great capacity
for imaginative distortion, that there was a
lukewarm type, one that set into white ricotta, and
one that was pliable when it curdled, and one that
was hard and opaque because of the lead and tin in
the stone pavements of the streets and in the earth
around the trees.

The underground rivulets of milk, which actually were very few, surfacing like springs in low-lying places, whitened the donkey watermelons, which exploded on contact, and the capers, over which the warm liquid gurgled.

We noticed that the children unconsciously invented neologisms to talk to each other. One would say: "O Turi, don't you see how the walls and the streets are milkening?"

And another would say: "O Peppi, the town is goating today! Further up it is chickening with musical eggs!"

Sinus continued to have his dark moods, during which he talked to me about, or better, gave me to understand that he intended to create, a mono-individual who would revive in himself the vital rhythms of all those who had passed away, but he would not say anything else. In spite of the worry he gave me with these strange ideas, we succeeded in establishing that the language of Zebulonia added Greek derivatives and archaic elements of Siculian, Sicanian, Byzantine, Arabic, Catalan, and French origin to an original Latin base. Sinus also wanted to study the family names of Zebulonia, like Margarone, Yaluna, Bonaviri, Sudano, Casaccio, Bellino, Privitera, Símili, Ballarò, Lauria, etc., and through them to determine how the ethnic groups had formed and dissolved through blood lines, and in the open air through the seasons, and through galactic cycles and vast gulfs of neutrons.

In the children the layering of verbal experiences was more evident, as perhaps they absorbed language and sound from the old people who were left. Thus, instead of fava they said *faba, hordeum* instead of barley, *spelunca* for grotto, *zona* for belt or coiled spring. Finally "sunset" became "sun's sorrow," and "I did" became *fhefhàked*.

It was a joyous play of words mixed with the braying of wandering donkeys, the wailing cries of goats, the piping of chickens, and Saturnian verses that the old people composed in the idleness in which they were compelled to live.

The roosters, too, were numerous, followed by groups of hens. They crowed everywhere, even on the roofs, as we mentioned. Their feathers had developed stronger colors, the red granulation of their combs was gaudy, their crowing was thunder igniting the last sulphurous surges of summer waning that October over the numberless crocuses that bloomed on the highlands.

Walking around in order to establish the layout of the streets where we were collecting different terms, we found ourselves in the steep quarter called Centímolo. It was made up of old houses and hovels lost in underground alleys.

"Oh," I asked Yaluna, "didn't all those adopted idiots once live here?"

"Yes, Ariete. They still do, but they've grown old."

We saw a number of them, who had climbed the stairs from their underground hovels all the way up to the street and now rested their crossed arms on its stones.

"There they are," Yaluna said.

Down in those buried rooms you could see their ancient adoptive mothers asleep under the electric lights, in little chairs darkened by evening.

"In the ninth century A.D.," I explained to Sinus, "together with the Arabs, the Jews arrived in this quarter. Their writing, as it was possible to establish from stones unearthed by earthquakes on which aphorisms were inscribed, went from right to left."

"Go on, Ariete, go on."

"It must have been a small colony kept in eternal subjection by the dominant groups, the Normans, the Spaniards, and the French. They must have been unable to find steady agricultural employment, since they got by chiefly with makeshift jobs, temporary farm work, or the sale of unleavened bread on feast days. From generation to generation they handed down psalms, prayers, ritual lamentations. Their religious practices and their concepts were derived indirectly from the Talmud. Their names also were of Jewish origin: Jacob, Moses, Zeraima, Emmanuel, Joseph, Isaac, Maria, Raphaela, Zachary. The Municipality of Zebulonia called the most crooked alley of that quarter Jews' Street. Perhaps they brought syphilis with them, because their poets wrote syphilographic poems listing medications containing mercury salts; but above all else in this dwindling group an obsession with sin and remorse persisted. Their very houses, unlike those of others, were low, with underground exits; some even communicated with the cisterns. They loved midnight, which they considered the day's watershed; at that hour they interrupted their sleep to pray in the endless darkness and, prey to fear, imagined that they saw the avenging angel in the incandescence that reached all the way to their half-buried hovels from the twisting patterns of the meteors." Sinus listened to me in silence while I informed him of the customs of the Zebulonian Jews, adding that in the spring, when the arid peaks flowered sweetly, those Jews walked along the paths of the nearby fields reciting the Song of Songs in unison.

All this was in tune with their adoption of the idiots and the deformed, in whom they found, as it were, the physical projection of life's corruption and the oceanic roar of poverty.

"Oh, d'you see?" Yaluna went on, pointing to the idiots, who shouted incomprehensible words to us from slobbering mouths, their faces vacant, worries heavy on their eyelids. Most of them were playing with the shadows that fell from rocks and balconies.

"Wretched, unlucky ones," Yaluna continued. "Nobody would want them if it weren't for those stepmothers of theirs whom evening has caught in the spiral of sleep."

Their hands were a dirty yellow, white in the creases of the palms. Their fingers molded sounds, figures, imaginary movements of objects. Some were playing with the droppings of goats and donkeys, with the excrement of chickens and with their own feces. They made little snakes from it, human faces, shiny fruits, buns, tree-like forms in which the *negra escuridad* from the valley below thickened.

"They are looking for fruit and light!" sighed Yaluna who stood near us. "We bring them dried figs and snails from time to time."

The idiots gradually became accustomed to our presence, so that they eyed us less malevolently, intent on creating people from feces.

"What are you doing? What are you doing?" Yaluna cried to them. For a moment they looked at us stupidly. A rooster crowed on top of a chimney, and from everywhere other roosters answered him.

Sinus told me that Ida Melange in her little treatise *De amore mutatis mutandis* had dedicated a page to fecal matter. Here it is: "God forgive me! but to achieve a comprehensive vision one must also speak about feces, which contain the great principles of the world: the fragile, the mobile, the unattainable, the cylindrical, the putrid, the microbic, the abject. Properly handled, they flash, sulphurize, carbonize, aureize, they contain rustling winds, and cold, warm, and sonorous elements. Every man is mirrored there in vaporous lightness, in heaviness, in calibrated circles; that is, you may find in them the man of letters, the doctor, the worker, the bookkeeper, the trade-unionist. Their colors represent our desires: yellow, like fire and little flames that rise upward, suggests the insecure man who follows the deceptive impulses of the soul; green, like broad verdant river banks, expresses an inclination for painting, abundance of biliverdin, and the curved symbols of geometry; fiery red tells us that the man (or woman) sees in atmospheric phenomena the embrace of earth and sky. Today, to advance this kind of research, artificial feces are produced."

Sinus told me that the origin of life must be sought in the fracture-points of things, that is, in the seismic faults, where a surface cracks, where it folds in on itself, and in the abyss.

"The idiots and your peasants who, by swallowing waves, create time, are the principal elements of sensory space in the process of formation. The vital principle resides in holes in the ground, in deposits of earth, in astral vortices. One must look to a new geometry. The real point of all this is found in cemeteries, which are the greatest inverted vertex of life. Why not draw spirits from the juices of the dead?"

In posing this question, the psychiatrist had a flash of madness in his eyes, which aroused in me the suspicion that he suffered from an intermittent delirium of perpetual desire for the ultimate principle. That is, he was straying from the technical-informational side of the research we had been assigned.

VIII

On August 11th, a month after our arrival, our inquiry became more complicated. In the locality of Nicchiara a peasant was found hanging from an oak. Strange that the suicide, a peasant of about seventy, had chosen such a high branch to hang himself, on that luminous morning. Within a few days similar cases occurred at Vilardo, Trezzito, Fiumecaldo, down at Pozzillo, at Corvo, Vallenuova, in the carob groves, at Saraceni, and Ruccuvè. They hanged themselves from the highest branches of olive trees and oaks, from the few elms and cypresses, from almond and fig trees. They were exposed, according to the hour, to various solar currents.

"Why is this happening?" we asked Yaluna, who followed us whenever she could.

"Oh, my children, what better place than up there? Above the dense foliage of the trees, you see everything clearly. At least they enjoy the light. Who do you expect to be happy any more in our town?"

"You're right," Sinus agreed. "If you look from below, every corpse looks like a black line suspended (or so it seems) from the vault of the sky."

We were all amazed by the dark sense of composure that emanated from the hanged men; like the composure of our Aunt Pipí, my brother Timor, who, in the photograph taken after her death, with a lit candle at her side and a big handkerchief restraining her jaw, seems cut off from the world, no longer listening to the growth of the crimson carnations she cultivated on her balconies, but headed ineluctably toward the rotating earth's regions of disintegration.

Sinus explained that series of suicides by the profound changes that had occurred in the space around the people of Zebulonia. That is, their olfactory space had no fragrant breezes, but had become a simple flow of dry air. It was no longer a swarm of fragrant particles, but a rigid circle.

"Hmm, yes," I mused.

"Their acoustic space," Mario Sinus continued, "lacking songbirds, buzzing wasps, and the sing-song chants of the past, has moved toward night with owls and clocks. Their visual space, Ariete, no longer extends over riverbanks, wheatfields, and orchards loaded with fruit. It has shrunk. You can hold it in your fist. If we like we can render these things in graphs. Olfactory space is concentric, given the circular expansion of the odorbearing particles emitted by arboreal powders. Acoustic space is like a sea that envelops us, and, when harmonious, it cradles us in horned and sighing sounds."

For my friend, the most profound space is the tactile, which, created by stratified sensations diffused over the entire body, gives us the geometrical sense of what surrounds us. The skin, according to Sinus, is the first thinking system, that is, it accumulates idea-memories in the epithelium, quantifying them in the brain, for all time, through the paths of the nerves and the body's fluids.

Yaluna observed, sighing, that so many things had changed: "You are alone, today. In the past if somebody died, the neighbors came, laid him out, wept for him with old expressions that freed us from grief. If the deceased had been a cabinet-maker, they put planes, hammers, fragrant boards at his feet. They did the same for the masons, the potters, the snake-hunters,* the violin players. If a man had a hard time dying, the sorcerer Abrucàl came, touching him with sardonyx and with his hands, he gave the dying man energy for a moment and helped him with litanies to lower himself into the void of death, which, as you know, is a place of dark rocks where no asphodels bloom."

The suicides usually used rope, which, made as it is of plants, has softness, fibrous texture, and a translucent gentleness that counsels goodness.

It was discovered that the women among them threw themselves into the cisterns, perhaps because they were haunted by the light, which might reveal the recesses of their soul. According to the psychiatrist, they were melancholy types, very reserved, quick to shut themselves in their houses as sunset faded. Drawn out with big hooks, they were enormous from the water, with protruding bellies. From the cisterns in that moment came the sound of deep waters. Some of the suicides had darkened eyes, their breasts pierced by crabs, some had bats at their nipples. Being female, they were adorned with rings, buckles, stones shaped like fish, whistles, silk veils. Some put the image of Saint Agrippina, the patron saint of the town, around their necks.

Because Zebulonia had many cisterns that communicated with each other through channels in the rock and mud that permeated the walls between them, underground streams of rainwater formed that favored the growth of little plants along the walls. Thus fleshy euphorbias prospered, little cypresses that caused blisters and sneezes if touched, and wild figs, which in that period bore glassy, snow-white fruits called *ficalbi,* whose ripening depended on the moonlight reflected in those wells by special mirrors. They wrapped the bodies of those wretched women in woody tentacles and crowns of sea-green, hairy figs, so that the women looked as if they had bracts for eyelids, blanched leaves for hands, and white branching along their spines.

Our encounter with death did not stop there. As autumn approached, the deaths of children increased, of the littlest ones entrusted by the emigrants to their grandparents and closest relatives. According to Mario Sinus, already unhinged by the wild idea of the mega-human he was pursuing, it was, more than malnutrition and the common childhood diseases, a question of a disintegration of the common sphere of affection, to which children are very sensitive. The mothers were far away, in fact, gone to foreign lands because they no longer believed that boiled wheat sweetened with honey, fava beans, and bread with bread and nothing else on it, could be enough to satisfy hunger and permit the normal growth of the body. Among the old people who remained, ancient funeral rites surfaced (ones that my mother, for instance, remembered), traceable to the many ethical-historical strata that had built up over so many centuries in Zebulonia. To the sense of the divine embodied in an unchanging ethos derived from the benevolent justice brought by the Immortals from their perilunar skies, Fear was opposed – an actual personification,

tragic in a mythic sense, changing in certain cases
into Terror, which could be exorcised only by a
flood of tears and contact with the stony earth of
Zebulonia.

The children were kept in the house for three
days and only on Wednesdays, it was decreed, were
they to be buried. To make those little corpses
look prettier, they were sprinkled with golden
powders. Against the established norms of inter-
ment procedures, which no authority in Zebulonia
could enforce any longer, they were laid in baskets
lined with artemisia, cypress branches, and purple
brocade. Because of the Christian sentiments of the
Zebulonians, they were taken first (the grandfather
carried a dead girl, the grandmother a boy) to the
Church of Saint Agrippina, the Roman patron saint
of the town. Her statue is attributed to Archifel of
Kalàt-Yeròn, who is supposed to have done it in
1519. She has the angular face of a Norman girl,
but the sad eyes of the Zebulonians, a cross in her
right hand, and in her left a castle with caves
leading to a labyrinth.

In the church carpets were displayed, capes,
mantles, monstrances, jeweled crowns, an altar
frontal of raw silk, shining icons between the
columns. It was a joy of the mind and of the eyes
as well, for the candles on the galleries, cornices,
and pulpits made it possible to admire the frescoes
of Sebastiano Monaco who conceived and painted
them in honor of the conveyance of the remains of
the saint from Rome, where Valerian was emperor,
to the territory of Zebulonia.

But the most emotional part of the ceremony
took place at the Pietre Nere where, before dark,
those processions converged from the alleys with

the dead children in their baskets. Here on the stony slopes there stands, as the name of the area indicates, a boulder from which copper, mercury, and tears trickle. Friar Onorio and the other two monks, who were invited for the occasion, maintained that the boulder was the remains of a meteorite, which had brought with it the celestial frosts. The Zebulonians thought that the god of the poor took refuge under that slab when fairness and goodness were lacking in people's souls.

"It is a cross of several profound traditions and religions," Sinus sighed, when the parents gave permission for us to be present at that ceremony.

People bowed deeply and reverently laid leafy branches, salt, and wheat on the great rock. The baskets with the dead children were arranged in a circle around that meteoric relic. Just as the sun was setting on the rocky outline of the mountains, the friars unfolded an embroidered cloth that with its brightly colored wildflowers and its emeralds arranged like the stars of Ursa Major reflected a dazzling light on the mountain rocks.

Mercurio was present at these funeral rites. As he played his clarinet he turned in all directions, to all the nearby valleys. His slow music, repeating its lowest notes, mingled with the words of the old women's prayers. It was said (but this hardly seemed true to us) that the crows flying through those gorges, the blackbirds, the wild doves, the solitary jays followed both the music and the wailing, and in the morning, as soon as dawn, rubbing her eyes, opened over the earth, they imitated those rhythms in their warbling, whistling, cooing, piping, as did the chirping of sparrows in their smooth flight.

107

In a chalice with a graceful design of tall slender figures, Friar Onorio gave the people green water to drink, which as we know he drew from cypresses, trees of great longevity that enclose in themselves the principle of long life.

Some water was allowed to drip on the dead children so that their eyelids would be wet with it. The deaths of those children had increased to twenty-two in only twenty days, just when the pomegranates were dropping both foliage and unharvested fruits. The Zebulonians who were left, in order that the last spark of life might linger in the eyes, ears, and tongues of those little bodies, were possessed by their innocent passion for sweets. In every house, with sugar, honey, flour, milk, the juices of cypress and rue, they made sweets shaped like little bottles of pink syrup, horses, fish, and from royal paste apples, medlars, sycamore fruits, lul-daghelí, prickly pears. Each fruit was a different color. They made many kinds of nougat, as on the feast of Saint Agrippina: fava bean nougat fragrant with cinnamon, filbert nougat coated with honey from ground-bees, almond nougat cut into rectangles, or shaped like hearts, praying hands, branches, and magic wands.

And, further, since death had arrived in Zebulonia in such a crushing form, like an unforeseen fatality, perhaps because of the change that the earth's rotation undergoes in October, the peasant women who had remained threw salt everywhere to purify the town. They kept a supply of it in jugs ranged along the walls of the house. It whitened the alleys where children ate it by the handful to sharpen their sight and alleviate their hunger. From the countryside sparrows and blackbirds came to peck at it. At night the women of Zebulonia went around with lamps lit to kindle rays from the salt very similar to those of the moon, so that a luminous veil stretched over Zebulonia. And some paralytic old woman would ask: "What is it? Is the comet Onorina coming?" From the refraction of the chloride salt, the exhalations of which passed through the breaches in the walls, a haze of blue arose that expanded in great sweeping circles and vanished in the gorges. The clay of Saint Agrippina, collected for this purpose from under the church in the grotto where the remains of the saint lie, was spread together with the rocksalt. Rocksalt is known to avert lightning, mitigate sickness, and sharpen the mind, while seasalt diminishes hunger, favors rain, and makes the singing of birds melodious.

The old men, in memory of the long-gone work of the fields, busied themselves filling the alleys, the roofs, the little trees on the rocky slopes nearby, with scythes, pitchforks, hayforks, hoes, picks, and some of the large reddish umbrellas peasants use. Some spicy food was also prepared, like salted ricotta dried in the sun, eggplants, and cheeses, to be placed together with the sweets on the cypresses and in the hands of the angels in the cemetery.

Perhaps it was a way of making up for a few days for the hunger the children were still suffering in Zebulonia, where sometimes (as in bygone days that I remember well) there was only bread for them to eat, together with thin slices of other bread, which they said was cheese. But their usual diet was fava beans, ricotta, a little fruit, and games that replaced the hunger for more food.

This storm of confectionery on the mournful occasions of death was whipped up further in the old women by the vivid memory of both the children and the sweets. They made necklaces with poppyseeds too, bracelets of figs strung with bayleaves, and eggs baked in buns.

Everything was carried to the cemetery on cloths of finest byssus and laid on the tombs of the dead little ones. Since in those days there was a full moon whose light came down from the mountains in long unbroken rays, the cemetery had become a sparkling river of sugar and honey. Nobody ate them. For they believed that the children would emerge from the earth and, blowing their trumpets, driving away the stagnant vapors, feed on those sweets. On one side, on the Cyclops' Walls, their relatives, the moonlight at their backs, cast their shadows down the slopes of the cemetery. It was a strange ceremony, nor did anybody remember a similar occurrence, except in the oral tradition of the funeral chants. At any rate they expected (Sinus shook his head) that, charmed by the sweet smells and the light, those little Zebulonians, freeing themselves from the deadly vapors and the mystery of the world beyond this life, through an intrinsic prerogative of their flesh, would reappear, to worship poverty and the god and to tell us that they had prevailed over nothingness.

I realized that in my townspeople, in accord with their emotions, manifestations of Orphism were reappearing, Anassimandrian principles, and belief in a luminous metamorphosis of all things.

IX

Mario Sinus was to suffer from this synthesis of religious beliefs so natural to the Zebulonians. My poor friend's rational principles did not permit him to see ambiguity in human behavior, nor in the dawn, nor in Zebulonia's pale bird of sleep. He intended to direct his attention to this in a short work entitled *Ars somniandi*. He maintained that in the past the oneiric activity of my townspeople had been minimal because of the great weariness that overwhelmed them, in their fatigue, at the end of the day, while now it was fuller and more complex because they were sailing on a sea of closed, blackened memories, which could not burgeon again in their distant children. To Sinus dreaming was a kind of archaic thinking, the first river, that is, which generates the network of thought. According to him, one could determine dreams beforehand. It would be enough to record the major emotional waves of the day or of preceding days, and allow the imagination to stabilize memories still in flux, for those waves to reappear in one's dreams, which by now were fraught with images of death, anxieties, a disturbing sharpness of smells, a desire to turn back and lose oneself in fields of rustling wheat.

I began to see my friend more rarely. Even Yaluna would ask: "Where's the professor gone? It seems to me that he's getting lost trying too hard to enter the mysteries of Zebulonia."

He frequented the monastery of the Capuchins, enchanted by the grandfather clock, which announced every hour that time flies irrevocably, and passed his time reading (an escape from solitude). Perhaps Friar Onorio instructed him in the heraldic history of the monastery and the idea of immortality to which he aspired, grinding lenses and preparing a new telescope with which he intended to resume his exploration of the galaxies, from which he was expecting an extraordinary event. With small lenses he studied his hands, the capillary veins, the cells, as if he really hoped to penetrate the depth of his own being. It was said that Mercurio enlivened their days by playing his clarinet in the monastery. He relieved the torments of those old men and the disturbing lunacies of Sinus who, among other things, in agreement with Father Onorio (as you tell me, brother Timor), maintained that there is not just one death, but that in the course of our life there are fleeting moments in which our vital current stops, interrupted for fractions of a second before it starts to flow again. And this rapid submersion in the river of mortality is necessary in order to regain life.

The fact is, I saw my friend for the last time on October 14. I asked around town, I searched for him, but I was completely unsuccessful, so that finally I informed the public prosecutor at Kalàt-Yeròn. The disappearance of Mario Sinus caused me problems that I would call infinite, were it not that only the universe in its vast extension is infinite.

Ida Melange, whom I never got to know, inquired as a representative of the Department of Public Health whether the major points of our inquiry were already established and whether the mystery of the ethnopsychiatrist could be explained by his acute mental disorders, especially since in October the moonlight hardens in the brooks, and the planets cast their longest shadows on the earth. In addition she asked me whether in Sinus the relationship that ordinarily exists in every person's psyche between the parts of the body and its totality had been interrupted. They were certainly unusual questions. For its part the Office of the Public Prosecutor of Kalàt-Yeròn, in Decree No. 1377/12/CT, ordered that all contradictions be clarified so that a proper indictment could be issued against whomever was at fault. Some technical consultants were named, among whom one, a geologist, established that the summit on which the cemetery stood was the mouth of an extinct volcano.

This consultant based his report on two authoritative sources. One was the book by the Arab Ibn 'al Atîr (d. 1233 A.D.) who wrote: "Al Hasan 'ibn 'al 'Abbas, governor of the island, after his bands raided the countryside, spoiled the crops and cut down the trees, hid grain and precious booty in the innumerable caves below Zebulonia."

The other, more accurate source was the conclusion arrived at, after adequate assessments, by the Volcanological Observatory at Càtana, which wrote in issue No. 1757 of its *Bulletin*: "The rocky ledge that extends north and west under the town of Zebulonia, formerly used for the pasture of ovines because of its abundance of sheepgrass, and today as sacred ground for the dead, because of its volcanic nature and the seismic collapses to which it has been subject, is riddled in all directions with

caverns and a maze of tunnels. Examining it with
the proper instruments we have found lapilli, green
spinelles resembling flowers, porphyry, and, in the
gleaming smoky darkness, two Roman swords,
eight Saracen scimitars, three Norman broad
swords, and, embedded in the seams of lava, a
bronze incense burner, a goblet depicting Allâh
with skyblue gems for eyes, embalmed mammon
cats, and several parchments with kufic inscriptions
that speak of the division, or tmesis, of the world
into two parts: the earth and the anti-earth."

These findings were easily explained by the
well-known trafficking down there of brigands,
hermits, rebellious vassals, all sorts of soldiers,
and tiny nocturnal lights from the Zodiac.

Leaving the search for Sinus aside for a moment,
it must be said that another problem arose for me,
that is, the decline of 'Alqama's condition. With
threads of the dim light she loved, the young
woman drew the profile of her father again and
again on the walls in amaranth purple. In a short
time she was doing this obsessively, reproducing
sketches of the paternal face on the floor, on her
clothes, on dolls, on the streaming reverberation of
the sunset itself. She often resorted to monologues,
at which the Zebulonians are masters, but while
they generally deal with perplexities, worries,
axioms, 'Alqama, lovely as her face and gestures
were, unravelled slow words, twisted in mournful
enigmas, accented by sad dances and tears. It
seemed to me that she had returned to some dark,
primitive chaos.

In vain Yaluna tried to rouse some response in
her by bringing her baskets of snails, raisins, and
rue. "Take it, 'Alqama, take it," she would say.

The neighbors, to help her free herself from those fixations, made her look at her own image in a bucket of water, told her fables, lit a fire in the street so that she could watch the flames and flying sparks. Mercurio was called for too, but nobody succeeded in finding the boy, who appeared to have followed Mario Sinus into the labyrinth.

"Ariete, do you think she will recover?" Yaluna would ask me, sighing.

'Alqama in certain moments assumed the position of a sleeper, thinking she could turn to stone to save herself from the world around her. Very soon she was prey to other uncontrollable phobias.

The girl felt she had been left at the mercy of dark, deep forces and was being sucked in by whatever was around her. So she filled the cracks in her few pieces of furniture, the holes in the walls, and everything round with paper and parietaria. From what I was able to understand ("O my God," Yaluna would comment, "how weird!"), 'Alqama was afraid of being dispersed outward as sound, light, and bursts of sparks when she was caught in the solar vortex reflected by the peaks of the Arcura. She was afraid she would lose her identity. She was even afraid of the eyes of her few visitors, thinking that the high luminous lines streaming from their corneas could entrap and swallow her up. All that was circular had become to her a spheric universe unto itself that absorbed all thoughts, physical structures, the loveliness of youth. The dissociation in the young woman had increased to the point that one afternoon, frightened even by the mounting ripples of the evening, she disappeared.

It was Yaluna who guessed that 'Alqama had made off before I decided to have her committed.

Some of her neighbors, on our insistence, told us that she had run away wearing a silk dress with gold threads, because the glittering that emanated from her body could not be explained otherwise.

Since we had not succeeded in discovering anything about the fate of my mother Algazèlia and her group, the inquiry had become more complicated; I was by now taking very little interest in it, despite the insistent entreaties of Ida Melange. My situation before the law was becoming ambiguous as well, for the authorities in charge were intent on clarifying the affair conclusively, while the first tiniest rivulets and channels of water were reappearing in the countryside, running toward the shade of the northern slopes before they could dry up.

Could Friar Onorio help me? He received me saying: "My son, how can I do it?"

As the three monks prayed in the temple they modified their voices, knowing that each sound must be given its own weight, curvature, and rhythm. Like all the old people of Zebulonia, they had the problem of passing their days without extending them into the immediate future. That is, they had to find a state of mind through which they could dissolve themselves in the smallest space.

"We have become masters at this," Friar Onorio explained, while the light in the stained glass of the nave grew rosy. "In line with the principle, in which nobody today believes, that any apparently primordial element splits in two, and again in two, and on and on in an infinite sequence of particles, which of course will never end, we do the same with our thoughts."

The friar explained that there in the temple, in the dark of the night, they prayed in order to enter themselves, along the points of a chain of ideas, until they found themselves pulsating with cosmic time, far, that is, from ordinary events. I realized that the friars were pursuing an insane consubstantiality with the logos and with the chronotope with which they identified, detached from their own bodies. In a certain sense they used the technique of all the old people of Zebulonia, who stay motionless behind windows and balconies, as my Uncle Michele and Aunt Pipí had also done, lost in an absolute unity of mind and body, so that the movement of their thought was entangled in the curving skeins of forgetfulness.

In any case I succeeded in convincing Father Onorio to take me into the vault that extended across the entire crater under the cemetery.

"You must know," he told me when we were down in the bowels of the earth, "that Sinus, gathering the essence of the corpses, or *spiritus mummialis,* and infusing it into his own seed, was trying to create an immortal being in whose freedom from the bonds of time he would have enjoyed the blessed condition of the gods. In this respect his view of life was opposed to ours. We find god in the pepper plant, the fava bean, the papyrus, the silfio.* Oh don't you see the little silfio plants?"

We were in the first passage of the labyrinth, where the refracted daylight still reached in a yellowish pallor. On either side that umbellifera grew, with abundant roots and cordiform seeds, some like little pendulous hearts.

"You know, Ariete," Friar Onorio told me, "the stem, when cooked, is called 'god's branch' because of its savory sweetness. From the leaves a juice is pressed that can be used in cooking and in many prescriptions for ailments."

The friar even insisted that he had found seeds of silfio enclosed in particles of the meteor that had fallen at the Pietre Nere because that fragrant plant, which combined with honey and juices pressed from cypress foliage increased the span of life appreciably, had disappeared for centuries from Cyrenaica and the Sahara Desert. It had been used by Hippocrates and Dioscorides, and mention of it has come down to us from Pliny the Elder and Apicius himself, but the only historical datum we have is from the high relief on the chalice of King Arcesilaus.

The air in that place was particularly fragrant because of the silfio, which no longer grew anywhere on earth. But as we went on past niches and tunnels, we found ourselves in darkness, barely illuminated by our flashlight.

The old man walked behind me, his head low. How could I respond if he went on extolling these imponderables and his own strange, morbid delusions?

"Your friend," he told me, "made a mistake encasing himself in the darkness of the dead without having studied its nature first. He often came down here with me."

"Do you think he has disappeared among all these caves?"

"What can I tell you? As you know, I am perfecting some lenses to study celestial phenomena. Everything comes from the heavens, including (perhaps from a star beyond the solar system) the seed of the silfio. I could not follow your friend wherever he went. As I told you, he should have studied the darkness of the dead first."

"What do you mean, Friar Onorio?"

"Listen to me, Ariete (Oh why did you leave us when doctors are so few here?). The first darkness that forms around a corpse is diaphanous, being an image projected by the dead person. Then, when the conformation of the body disintegrates, that darkness changes. Issuing from the mouth of the dead, it is absorbed by the nearby stones. Finally, when the so-called *spiritus mummialis* emerges from the dead, it darkens in the roots that you can see hanging above our heads. Do you see?" he added, "Those woody scales are from the roots of the cypresses. You can touch them. These over here – did you notice them? – are from laurels and giant mushrooms that grow throughout the cemetery."

In the vault of a cave, where our voices became almost inaudible, as if sucked upward, various plants could be seen, upside down, in chthonian growth: small cinerarias with cerulean fruits, a pomegranate with deep red fruits, plum trees, wild figs, a small spicebush, black olives. If we inadvertently touched them as we passed, berries, leaves, and figs fell all around us.

Later we found ourselves in a sequence of caves that branched into each other through funnels, narrowing passages, unexpected openings.

"Above us," the friar told me, "there is a layer of selenium, shiny and transparent. We can see who is buried up there. And it's here I come when I'm dejected, if I grow melancholy, Ariete."

I looked up, undeniably amazed at what I saw – great slabs of variegated porphyry and quartz of a vitreous brilliance, with paired crystals in which the polarized beam of our flashlight turned on itself. From a direction I could not determine, in a vibration of stone, I heard what I thought was a clarinet. Was it Mercurio perhaps, who had followed Sinus into those winding caves?

"Up here," the old man went on, "the mothers of Zebulonia are buried. You can see the corpses, strangely iridescent in the sinuous play of the light."

It was a light flashed from the blades of cold, tender hands, of cinquefoil shadows, of robes and drapery that enfolded those bodies. Their eyes were like purple amethyst.

"Come," the friar said, "don't stand there spellbound, we have more walking to do."

With the reflections, you could see better now. Two hundred and twenty steps further on, above a translucent cavern, we saw the bodies of the peasants overwhelmed by reefs of fava beans that grew wild around them together with delectable licorice plants and a host of green pods that were actually growing upside down.

"If we were to stay longer we'd be able to see, at the feet of the olive trees, the threefold dreams of the dead who lie here."

Following Friar Onorio, somehow I found myself under the chapel of the master craftsmen. In the hyacinth rocks mottled with purple you could distinguish cabinetmakers, masons, stonecutters, tailors, shoemakers.

"Draw in the thoughts, the goodness, and the burning water that oozes from the undercemetery in the form of bioplasma," the monk said. His oracular mode of expression did not astonish me, for I felt united, through the past and the future, with that vault of artisans who, because of some granules of gold trapped in the quartz aggregate, suddenly shone brightly. "I am used to this brilliance," the old man sighed.

Through a funnel we entered a cavern still full of pumice, lapilli, and volcanic little geodes; in a matrix of red porphyry that stretched over our heads in magmatic slabs, I saw the dead children. They had bonnets and gingham clothes on, sulphur in their hands, and in their arms flowers and leaves still green because of the moist earth. Some were already enclosed in those igneous rocks that enfolded their bodies like generous breasts.

"Link the thought of the dead," Father Onorio suggested, "to the intelligence of the world, as your friend Sinus did."

Some of the children had green lachrymatories under their eyes in case they should be seized by the need to cry; next to them, in a series of granite prisms, there were more corpses.

"Those are the magicians," the monk explained. "As you know, Zebulonia had many of them. They helped the dying to pass on without pain."

They were wrapped in capes and chimeras with staring eyes; they must have been buried in the most remote crescent of the cemetery.

"Absorb the bioplasma, absorb it," my guide said to me. "It oozes out and is dispersed down here in small particles."

121

Those magicians created moons with long white pepla that surrounded the perimeter of the cemetery.

"Do you see how brilliant their light is here?" said Friar Onorio. "The magicians create new regions of thought. Perhaps you believe, Ariete, because of your medical training, that death is the end. No, it's not so! No."

How could I have answered him? The wail of the clarinet grew louder, finding a thousand reverberations in those caves although it was impossible to determine where it came from.

"I'm leaving now," the old man told me. "I'm going back. The path gets uneven and I can't manage it any more. Whatever oozes from this tangle of caves is the pure essence of the corpses, containing the gravitons of antilife. Every living being is endowed with them. I have been looking into this too for many, many years, correlating it with the realms of the starry universe. If you break a leaf in half, Ariete, you will see a kind of shadow, a slight, residual trace of living spirit, where the half you must destroy to see the result is missing. Goodbye, Ariete!"

I cannot deny that, left alone, I was afraid. I walked for about an hour. Mercurio must have been following me, with his melodies, unwittingly. Under some limestone stalactites (anyone who wants to retrace my path should follow a course that runs south-east-east-west-west-south) I found a natural stairway of chalcedony and red-spattered lead that took me across an opening to the edge of a chasm. I leaned over. I saw an abyss filled (or so it seemed) in its immensity by an eye, because it was an eye, of a cloudy purple, its curved rim covered by a transparent membrane. Believe me, the eye looked infinite to me, and perhaps the chasm that Mario Sinus had found was infinite, where, by increasing his seed with the bioplasma of the dead of Zebulonia, he had been able to create that watery ocular well, the first essential element of the immortal being that my friend perhaps was not able to bring forth.

Nor do I believe that it was a question of optical illusions originating from the quartzes and the streams of mercury that issued from the surrounding rocks. That immense ocular wheel was clearly visible in its aqueous principle, but it did not yet have arms, a tongue, or a brain; instead, its spherical form mirrored its own light, at times steady, at times sparkling darkly. It was a limbless globe that concentrated in itself the empty pulsing of the spirits of the dead, the isotopes and the implosions of a primordial time in the process of formation.

I remembered Friar Onorio saying during our walk: "Ariete, the One that incorporates the fleeting essences of the dead bodies is the vortex that tends towards immobility, that is, towards immortality, where there are no spinning atoms, no memory."

I realized that Mario Sinus wanted to re-enter the timeflow of that boundless ocular bioplasma, in order to cross over then to an immortal condition. While the illusory contrasts of the dim light caused that sphere to absorb my enormous shadow, I heard again, far away and indistinct, the clarinet of Mercurio. Whom was he looking for in those labyrinths? Whom was he calling?

X

By way of a conclusion to this affair, a newspaper report on its involuted epilogue must be appended here.

"After his descent into the volcano, nothing certain could be established about Ariete. Some say they saw him in a field among clocks and models of pyramids intent on determining the ideal point where all people could converge; others maintained that while searching for the god of the poor he turned into grass; the public prosecutor at Kalàt-Yeròn condemned him by default, considering him a codefendant in a case of felonious assault perpetrated against the last group of living Zebulonians.

"Concerning the actual existence of this Ariete, there are many positive indications. In documents in the registry office of Zebulonia, which we have consulted, he is said to have been born around dawn on July 11, and baptized two months later, his godparents (by proxy, the aforesaid having emigrated to New York) being his uncle, Michele Rizzo, and his cousin, Maria Casaccio. It appears that he was an honest man, myopic, a great bread-eater, like all poor Zebulonians, reserved by nature, very affectionate to his two children, leading a rather solitary life; however, the judicial controversy in which he found himself involved determined that because of his cowardice not only did he fail to recognize the madness of Sinus, despite the fact that as a doctor he was the expert in charge, but even disappeared at the opportune moment to evade probable conviction. Traces of him remain on painted treetrunks, in ant hills, in the fabulous lul-daghelí, a shoot of which, blooming strangely in October, can be seen among the enormous stones that make up the Cyclops Wall.

"But the most unusual fact was the following. Since the Zebulonians have an innate tendency to blend the real and the imaginary to create plays, or forms that can be adapted for the theater, out of the uncertain destiny of Algazèlia and her friends, of Dolcissimo and his daughter, of Sinus and his friend Ariete, they created a hybrid of modern drama, religious ballad, mystery play, and grottesco theater, to express the malice, the ethical bent, and the tortuous convolutions of their mind. The work was performed in the public squares of Plaza Hermosa, Ganz, Ochiolà, Burchiaturo, Eubèa, Millestelle, in Atlantide, rich in sheepflocks, Kalàt-Yeròn (in spite of the public prosecutor), Diòclia, Fontania, rich in citrus, Palíca, and in Tesbia, from which you can see the valleys, the crags, the buttery plains of the moon. Various newspapers took notice of these things; we assure you that we have examined them all, although the most reliable testimony comes from the extremely cautious *Le Monde* (No. 34.777).

"They would erect a crude stage made of cinnamon wood, carpets woven in the past by the women of Zebulonia, aluminum foil, peacock feathers, and straw. It was lit by ordinary bulbs, or, if the owls were hooting, by river cattails. An enormous cave, painted to resemble a labyrinth, descended into a vast darkness attenuated by tiny lights that were nothing else, in those town squares, but ordinary starlight channeled onto the stage by mirrors.

"So as not to alter the structure of the play, we follow the example set by Sinus and Ariete in recording the song of emigration, and report the text here as a dramatic dialog, the way it was presented in Zebulonia."

A stage is set up in Piazza Buglio. The scenery, made of painted cardboard, depicts a labyrinth stage rear. Many old men in caps stand listening. From the balconies looking down on the square a few old women watch the play and from time to time collect snails from the damp walls. Among them is Aunt Ignazina, who watches through a crack in her balcony to escape notice, because she is the paternal aunt of Ariete.

Uncle Michele: Now that we have left behind the region of the waters, let us confront the trip through these rocks.
Yacomina, a child: Oh, aren't you hungry? My hunger pinches me, it bites me, it twists inside me.
Tèlefo, the Swordswallower: We have few provisions left: fava beans, chickpeas, and this cursed sun that burns as it sets.
Yacomina: And the goat?
Mother Algazèlia: We need it for the milk. White, the milk is. Walking so far in the yellow of the countryside, we have begun to forget colors.
Tèlefo: The goat is old. It is of little use. The milk it gives us is less than a cupful. Nor do we know what will become of us. At least we will remember the taste of meat.
Algazèlia: Seeing no milk we will forget white. Once the sun is high, there is nothing but sunlight.

The Chorus of Old Women: The goat is strong no longer. It bleats sadly and today, the 11th of October, we have no chickpeas, no pepper, no carts with painted panels. We are tired of all this walking, of all the children only Yacomina is left. A hundred thin veils cover our eyes. The goat is strong no longer.

Uncle Michele: So be it. Our hunger is strong. Let us put on bronze masks so that the animal will not see our faces. Killing is abominable.

(The goat is bound. It bleats. It shrieks. Covering their faces with masks, the group kills and quarters it. Some kindle a fire of dry branches. The chorus of old women cover their faces with their black shawls. The meat is basted with vinegar sprinkled from twigs of laurel; as the aroma rises, the cries of the goat seem to be heard in the distance still.)

Yacomina (having eaten abundantly of the meat): I am full. Uncle Michele, too. I can see it from his smooth brow. I would like a pallet of straw to sleep on.

Ops, the Violin Player: Let us not be overcome by the fatigue of repletion. We must continue our journey. I see no path, nor traces of a road. All the rocks are turning red, all the valleys and ranges of stone.

Yacomina: I see a cave. Why don't we encave ourselves, Uncle Michele? In there sleep will come and protect us with its bulwarks, and even our eyes will be silent.

Uncle Michele: What do you say, Zebulonians?

Tèlefo: Sleep will turn to darkness on our brows and lips. All that's left us now is sleep. We have lost honey, carob pods, cinnamon, and almonds. Our land produces them no longer.

The Chorus of Old Women: Praised be the goat. It saved us from hunger. Let prayers be raised to the goat. Its seed is in us, blood, liver, and marrow.

(Yacomina enters the cave first, followed by Uncle Michele and the old men.)

Tèlefo (outside, bends down to look in, fastening his swords to his belt. Then he asks): Is there sand or clay for us to sleep on?

Yacomina: Come in, swordswallower. The cave is deep, there is room for everyone. It seems to slope downward.

Uncle Michele (who entered with the child, once accustomed to the dim light): I do not understand whether it is a reluctant wind coming from the bottom of the cave, or a voice, or sleep coming on. *(Then he adds):* Let us go on, we must explore this place.

Ops (who carries a violin tuned by Mnémio the blind): Let's enter even if it is very dark. To give ourselves strength let us think of the dove in the wild olive and of the womb of the mother from whom the moon is born.

Uncle Michele: Let us light torches.

(All enter and begin their walk by the light of dim torches in the flickering glow of copper and garnet.)

Yacomina: Oh, but where does this cave lead?

Uncle Michele: Who has the goat's skull?

Tèlefo: I kept it in my sack.

Uncle Michele: Give it to me. I'll put an oil lamp in it. It will throw more light into dark corners.

Yacomina: Oh, how far down the cave slopes, how far! Don't you hear a kind of wailing?

(The lighted skull sheds a faint, diffused glow. They make two rounds of the cave and stop.)

Algazèlia: There is the sound of a human voice. It is weak; it fades away.

Uncle Michele: Be of good cheer. Someone is up ahead of us.

Yacomina: Oh, isn't there something in that protruding boulder? Shine the light on it.

(They all fall silent.)

Yacomina: You can hear something. Isn't it the cry of the dying goat that is reborn here in so many echoes?

The Chorus of Old Women: Perhaps it is the cry of the hawk that nests in here. Or the thunder of lava beaten by the wind. Blessed be every sound; it is not empty noise; even the heart has it, and Zebulonia when it trembles in an earthquake, even snails into which the chirping of sparrows bores, and our ruined palmgroves.

Yacomina: Come see, come see!

Uncle Michele: Your voice is fading. Where are you? Which direction must we take?

Yacomina: Is it a human being? His arms are immersed in the stone, his fingers seem made of obsidian. In his hands is a network of small roots. Oh, what is he telling me? He has inearthed himself.

Uncle Michele: Here we are.

Yacomina: It seems to me that it is...can it be...Dolcissimo?

Uncle Michele: How can one recognize him in such darkness? What can we do to free him?

The Chorus of Old Women: O Dolcissimo, our son! Your eyes still gleam with mint and thyme. Their flickering light is useless now. You are losing your body. Your mind is falling into the

vortex. Perhaps the sense of touch is still left to
you.

Algazèlia (gazes at the man by the light of the skull):
O Dolcissimo, you were searching for 'Alqama
in these places. For her sake a passion for the
waters seized you, for the Capricorn horses, for
the tuttifrutti tree.

Mnémio, the Blind Man: 'Alqama was the apex of
your soul. Touching you, I feel a tree with
numberless arms. But your wrists and forehead
are turning to stone. I have no eyes, but you,
Dolcissimo, are creating around you a vast
geometry of forms.

Uncle Michele: How can we help him? Give me
light with the skull.

The Chorus: Dolcissimo, all sound has ended for
you. But in its place you leave us poverty, which
invents the arts and teaches us wisdom.

Yacomina: Uncle Michele, why don't we uproot
him from the rock?

Uncle Michele (turning to the others): Do you think
we can free him from this tangle of underground
branching? From the garnet that has already
entered his flesh?

Yacomina: We can free his body if everyone helps.

(Dolcissimo still retains minimal ocular movement.)

Uncle Michele: What is shining there beside him?
Turn the goat's skull this way.

Yacomina: Oh, it's his rooster; it shines so brightly
it looks like gold. It is joined to Dolcissimo.

(The child touches it softly again and again.)

Algazèlia: It is the rooster Polieno that always
accompanied Dolcissimo. Accustomed as he
was to meditation, we learned from him that the
fear of death is vain.

Yacomina: It has turned to stone on Dolcissimo's shoulder. Why don't we free him from all that tangle of roots?

Ops: They have lost their senses, their passions, their body's pain; their present life is drawn from the atoms of plants.

Uncle Michele: Let's not stop to think about it. Let us free him, because he is one of our own.

(The old men dig into the floor of the cave with hoes and hammers and chisel the rock.)

Yacomina (realizing that the cave descends through many narrow passages): Oh, how many roads and paths! Stop a moment. Be quiet! Don't you hear some kind of sound?

(The peasants stop working for a moment.)

Tèlefo: The dying cry of the goat follows us. Don't you hear the boulders vibrate?

Ops: No, it is a musical instrument. Silence! It is a clarinet. Could it be Mercurio's? Is he also in these caves?

(It really was Mercurio, lost in the labyrinth, who was pursuing Sinus, calling to him with his music.)

Uncle Michele: Come on. Let's go on with our work. Why do you distract us, Yacomina?

(The group resumes its work, finally extricating the body of Dolcissimo from the numberless roots and the branching of copper and garnets around his body.)

Mnémio: Now let us praise all those who are dead. They lie above us in the cemetery. I hear their breathing. Let us praise Dolcissimo, now at the end of his life. Let us remind our eyelids of his daughter 'Alqama and the fragrant herbs of the earth of Zebulonia. Praise be to the clarinet of Mercurio, which channels light to us.

Algazèlia: Let us beat on the goat's skull, so that its hollow and its full may sound in harmony with Mercurio's clarinet and with the vibrations of our dead.

(Dolcissimo is completely freed from the surrounding earth.)

The Old Men: There, we have done it. We see no meadows, no wheat; which way do we go?

Yacomina: Oh, how hard the eyes of Dolcissimo are. They are made of stone. Yet shadows are moving across his face.

Uncle Michele: Let's go on with our journey, even if it is dark. Why turn back when in Zebulonia there are not even sunsets anymore? Forward! That way!

(The old men carry Dolcissimo, who no longer gives any sign of life.)

The Chorus: O Algazèlia, you have led us to these caves to look for your son Ariete! You are longing for him, waiting for him, linking him to the fever of your mind. With you we have searched for him in vain in the mildness of the waters, in the rue, in our dying race. Now you are trying to find him in the cry of the dying goat, in the rooster Polieno, in these places of death, in your gravedigger's heart.

Yacomina: This way, Uncle Michele, there is a path leading downward. You can't see the bottom.

Uncle Michele: The darkness is thickening. Give me the goat's skull to light up the labyrinth.

Mnémio: By touch I sense the darkness, it has different shapes. The music of Mercurio expands it around me.

Yacomina (touching Dolcissimo whom the old men are still carrying): Oh, how this dead man vibrates to the sound of the clarinet, his head, his chin, his hands!

Uncle Michele: Many echoes issue from the caves.

The Chorus of the Women: Dolcissimo is the god we have looked for throughout our land. He gave us back the desire for bread, for roots, for poverty. In these vast caverns the breath of our dead arrives like the wind. Knowledge exists no longer, nor waters.... Let us free our dead from their earthly memory. They are imprisoned in their tombs, but their arms reach far in these lava stones, making them glow. For us now the time has come to die.

Tèlefo: Yes, it is time to die. There is fear in our heels, our tongues are tied, in this mute earth all white is lost.

Uncle Michele: Come, let us press forward! No complaints. Let us not stop.

(Here we must note that 'Alqama, fearing that light might make her swing out from her body, had painted her black hair gold, her hands green, and holed herself up among the caves of the cemetery, where the planet Mars in its luminous passage makes wormwood sprout from its base. And here is what happened.)

Yacomina: Oh, Uncle Michele, a shadow is coming toward us.

Uncle Michele: Yacomina, you are seeing things!

Yacomina: Look, all of you. Look!

(It was 'Alqama. She looked at Dolcissimo but, crazed as she was, in that image of plant and stone she thought she saw the god of the poor.)

'Alqama: O god of the poor, as a child I saw you in the sacristy of the Capuchins, seated behind a

curtain. You looked at me with your silver eyes.
Now I see you motionless, turned to stone.

The Chorus of Women: 'Alqama, our daughter, we
have found you. Perhaps the god weeping in the
temple because he was abandoned by everyone is
your father Dolcissimo who has been searching
for the vital principles of the world.

*(The keening women form a circle around 'Alqama
who tries with her breath to restore vital feeling to her
father. She breathes into his mouth and nostrils.
Particles of fragrance swirl around them.)*

Ops: You want to bring your father into the light of
day again.

Uncle Michele: He who has turned to stone cannot
be reborn. Dolcissimo has been snared among
roots and stones too long. Let us press forward.

*'Alqama (continues to circle around her father. She
looks at his hands, already stone, his dimmed eyes,
his mouth closed forever. She notices the rooster
Polieno, also turned to stone):* O god of the poor!
How often I have seen you! I remember you and
the clouds, you and the circling sun, you and the
book of prayers.

Uncle Michele: Look at him more closely, despite
the darkness.

Ops: Don't you remember Dolcissimo?

*Yacomina (draws close to 'Alqama, pulls gently on
her skirt and murmurs):* It's your father. Don't
you have a father?

Uncle Michele: Let us leave her in her oblivion.
Perhaps it is better. Don't you think so?

*'Alqama (recognizing her father, she digs her hands
into her hair, griefstricken, then laughs, an
outburst of laughter. She falls silent again.*

Then): In what form do you come back to me? Don't you recognize me? It's me, 'Alqama.

Ops: He cannot recognize you any longer. He has fallen away from the edges of life.

'Alqama: O father, are you dead? Are you gone? Were you looking for me in these caves? *(She falls silent. She thinks she sees images of her father in the many shadows projected on the wall by the goat's skull.)* O father, how many shapes are you taking on in the labyrinth? I see you everywhere. And this music that comes from within? Is it calling you? Is it pulling you toward another shore? Don't leave me. Stay with 'Alqama once more. We'll look for nests together. We'll gather fragrant leaves. *(The young woman begins once again to breathe on his head, his eyes, his chin.)*

The Blackrobed Chorus: Breathe, breathe upon him, 'Alqama. Dolcissimo gave us fragrant herbs, pastured the flocks, set down his thoughts on the mountains of Arcura. Breathe, that pride may fall, that grief for the dead may be soothed, and the goats on the mountaintops give us milk again.

Ops: Closed in as we are here, we must absorb the vital essence of our dead to gain another life. Our months, our years are mist vanished from our senses. Only thus will we approach the fullness of Dolcissimo and move beyond mortal time.

Yacomina: Why go on grieving? Come! I have found a natural stairway that leads to a rocky ledge.

Tèlefo: Where are you, Yacomina?

Yacomina: Here, over here. Light the way with the goat's skull.

135

(The Zebulonians soon find themselves at the edge of a great precipice from which, hearing them, owls emerge, first in small groups, then in great swarms.)

Uncle Michele (leaning over): It is an underground lake that has sucked down all our water. Or is it a marsh that gathers the vital essence washed from the dead?

The Women: And our tears and those of the dead who are buried above us.

Yacomina: Oh, so many owls! They are still coming out, by the hundreds. Where do they roost? Careful! They might beat against us with their wings and make us fall into the abyss. Careful. Do all the owls of Zebulonia come from here then?

Tèlefo: It looks to me like an enormous eye. Don't you see a kind of membrane around the edges, opening and shutting?

Uncle Michele: What are vou saying, Tèlefo?

Ops: It is an eye. Don't you see? It shines at the center like an immense pupil. It hardly moves. It is immersed in nothingness and unconscious of itself.

Uncle Michele: What are you saying? Let's be careful with all these owls flying around.

Yacomina: Uncle Michele, don't you see a sort of shadow sailing in the lake?

Uncle Michele (looking): How can one be sure with this dim goat light?

Yacomina: It is. It's a man's body, I tell you.

(All gaze silently into the abyss.)

Ops: Yes, it is. The blinking of the eyelids carries him toward us.

Yacomina: O Algazèlia, it is Ariete, believe me.

Uncle Michele: Mad, you are driving me mad.

Algazèlia: O Ariete, my son, you are in the eye that rules all things, but you have lost the fire of life. There is nothing more for you now but this being into which the plasma flows. My son, I have searched for you through the valleys and plains, even in the springs and rivers!

Dolcissimo's Bearers: We have arrived at this vast pool. It reflects us all. It reflects you too, Dolcissimo.

(The Zebulonians lean over. 'Alqama continues to breathe upon her father's temples. The owls continue to fly, beating their rowing wings. Mercurio's clarinet is heard from every direction. All gaze and listen in silence.)

When the play was over, the evening had advanced over the roofs. Aunt Ignazina (who for months had had no peace because her family had been destroyed), had watched it from her semienclosed balcony so as not to be seen. At the end of the performance she appears to have exclaimed: "Can it be that my nephew Ariete has met with such an end? O god!"

Among the peasant women of Zebulonia, I also saw a very old woman called Yaluna making her way along the main street with a basket of snails in her hands, who said, wiping away her tears: "Oh, these poets, how many things they dream up! how many!"

XI

Two new events occurred that October: the appearance of the horses called "Capricorns," and the unusual increase in the number of shooting stars.

The former could not have sprung from the common equines of the peasants of Zebulonia because for their work in the fields they used hoes, scythes, or their bare hands; if they used any draught animals at all, they were gray donkeys called "blackies" and tawny donkeys called "rusties." Nor is it possible that the Capricorn horses descended from the horses of the big landowners because those were not thoroughbreds; they had stocky bodies and reddish manes.

The Capricorn horses, on the other hand, were notable for the white hair that grew around their hoofs, for their purple manes, and their remarkably pensive eyes. According to the hippologists, that breed had been brought into the island with the troops led by the Arab Ased, an educated young man, well-versed in the Koran, son of the cadi Ased-ibn-Forât-ibn-Sinâm; he landed in Sicily in 821 with ten thousand foot soldiers and seven hundred horses transported by two hundred ships that touched land near the stone quarries of Syracuse. He destroyed the Byzantines in the course of numerous encounters, but died badly wounded in 829. Decimated by the plague, his soldiers, to escape from Theodotus who was pursuing them, took refuge in the volcanic mountain of Zebulonia, which they called Qalàt Minàw; indeed, to escape discovery they sought out the labyrinths in which Sinus was lost.

The horses of Ased, left on their own, moved from the coast to the Iblean and Erean mountains, to the kind of barren land to which they were accustomed. In the warmth of those regions they had multiplied quickly, giving rise to a species of Capricorns that combined with their wildness a solitary nature tempered by an extremely gentle disposition. As those mountains had no woods or clear rivers, no blooming pomegranate or orange trees, they fed on the deliciously sweet bushes of the rocky slopes.

Arriving in Zebulonia in isolated groups at first, they left their numerous hoofprints in the clay. The oldest Zebulonians remembered those horses, called Capricorns because of two visible frontal protuberances and a striking resemblance to a billy goat from the rear. They were seen in the mountain passes and on the peaks where barley and spelt grew wild. Various groups of them took up stations in town and others within the perimeter of the cemetery, from which, to the astonishment of the custodian Margarone, dark waters full of sodium, iron, gold, mercury, and various saline spirits then flowed. These horses were given to fleeing from the night: in groups of about twenty-three they ran through plains and valleys after the sun as it withdrew behind the mountain ranges. Seeing those Capricorns moving through alleys and streets, the old people realized that they were thinking creatures attuned to the celestial order. Thus, when the Bears began to rise in the sky, the town was full of owls and Capricorn horses, both considered species capable of thought.

During that period the firmament of Zebulonia was crisscrossed by an exceptional number of meteorites. The Zebulonians who went up to their roofs to enjoy the warmth that had built up during the day in the rooftiles that October called to each other just loudly enough to be heard, pointing out all those shooting stars, which were drawn toward Zebulonia from their vast orbits in a great jet of sparks. Those that were not reduced to green gases by friction fell in great numbers on the hill of the cemetery where day by day the gravitational waves increased. The astronomers took note of the phenomenon, and in France, on October 17th, the aforementioned *Le Monde* discussed it. Some said that the prophecy of Father Onorio was coming true; he had foreseen the appearance of dust falling from the comet of von Biela-Secchi in the cul-de-sac formed when the earth is in line with Mercury at aphelion. The old monk had also spoken of a simultaneous fall of tectites that are produced by the impact of a meteorite on the lunar surface, from which point, because of the low orbital velocity of our satellite, they are ejected in fragments and hurled toward predictable zones on the earth.* That astral matter fell on the olive and the almond trees, catching at times in the forks of the branches. Blazing rocks reached the courtyards, the balconies, the tufts of parietaria that pervade the town. Some glittered, others were scalding hot, according to the old men who gathered them in crates to use for building material. The boys played with those stellar pebbles in place of the filberts they no longer had: throwing them to the ground by handfuls and sending them toward little holes they scooped out, with a rub of the thumb against the index finger. The girls did something similar, playing jacks with them, throwing them down and scooping them up rhythmically.

The phenomenon was truly intense, according to the graphs the astronomers drew from careful tabulations of that white rain. We cannot vouch for the truth of reports that hawks used those meteorites to strike the last snakes of autumn from on high, or that because the hens pecked at the shining fragments, these were later found in their eggs. It is certain that the sparrows, the crows, and the owls themselves carried those lunar pebbles to their empty nests to repair the holes in the woven grass.

The most imaginative of the Zebulonians said that the phenomenon was caused by the god of the poor (in whom nobody really believes today, since poverty no longer exists) who, rising from the depths of the earth into the highest reaches of space, wished to bid a visible farewell to the old, and to the oldest.

The fall of those stones lasted several days. In the towns of Ochiolà, Burchiaturo, Kalè Eubea, Palíca, and Kalàt-Yeròn, the peasants climbed the oak trees and the eucalyptus to enjoy the play of light, which, curving to the earth, enclosed distant Zebulonia in a brilliant circle.

August 1975-October 1977

NOTES

Page 1. *Zebulonia is the name used by Bonaviri in this novel for the fictionalized version of his home town of Mineo (Gr. Menàinon; Ar. Qalàt Minàw), a hilltop town southwest of Catania in Sicily which, under different names and fictionalized to varying degrees, is the setting for most of his novels and short stories. [Tr.n.]

Page 1. †Although today *siculo* as an adjective means "Sicilian," here as a noun and later as an adjective it refers not to the Sicilians but to the Siculi or Siculians, a pre-Roman population of Sicily inhabiting the east-central part of the island, while the Sicani or Sicanians inhabited its west-central portion. The Greeks colonized most of the eastern coast of the island, the Phoenicians from Carthage most of the western coast. The Arabs occupied Sicily in the eighth century. [Tr.n.]

Page 1. ‡A Greek-Sicilian historiographer, first century B.C. [Tr.n.]

Page 2. *Bonaviri explains that "gleaners" were people who actually supported themselves by gleaning, while almond pickers gathered and peddled almonds; people who peddled lemons in a lemon-producing region were, obviously, very indigent; stone gatherers were those who collected stones for anybody who needed them to build or repair stone walls. [Tr.n.]

Page 2. †An anagram of the name of the town of Camuti. [Tr.n.]

Page 3. *Anno Domini millesimo sexagesimo nonagesimo tertio. Die 11 Januarii 1693. In dicto die causa dicti terraemotus diruta fuit tota Civitas una cum omnibus Ecclesiis, et mortui sunt 2000 cives de quibus nulla fit mentio, et fuerunt sepulti sine pompa et sine exequiis; et aliqui homines, eadem de causa, post aliquas hebdomadas mortui fuerunt. [G.B.]

Page 3. †Solwan is really a kind of seashell in which water is given to lunatics to drink, to make them sane. Thus they know that time and space are infinite, so that Zebulonia is located at no fixed point of the universe and thus lives in boundless time. [G.B.]

Page 3. ‡While in English most words of a book title are usually capitalized, in Italian, Latin, etc., only the first word usually is. However, Bonaviri does not capitalize even the first word of many of the titles he mentions from here on, to suggest an approximation of a title rather than an exact one; however, all titles given here will retain the standard form of capitalization used in the particular language. [Tr.n.]

Page 4. *With Giovanni of Procida, Adinolfo and his uncle Alàimo were the guiding spirits of the uprising against the French in 1282, during the Sicilian Vespers. But, having had a falling out with the king of Spain, to whose land they had been taken, they were condemned to be thrown into the sea. Wrapped in their cloaks, they courageously threw themselves in, under the eyes of the soldiers. And the waves that wash along the coast of Spain where they perished tell those who know how to listen that the fifteen gold-haloed moons emerging from the sea in the great lunisolar year cannot quench the great longing for life of those heroes. [G.B.]

Page 9. *"Per qui si va, chi vuol andar per pace," Sinus says, quoting Dante a little freely; the text actually begins, "Quinci si va..." Purg. xxiv, 141. The translation is Lawrence Binyon's, *The Portable Dante* (New York: Viking, 1947). [Tr.n.]

Page 9. †The title gives the impression of authenticity, since it is made up of a well-known Latin title, *De amore (On love)* and a common expression, *mutatis mutandis* (appropriate changes having been made), but is nonsensical. [Tr.n.]

Page 21. *Massaro is the traditional title given to the overseer of a large farm in Sicily. [Tr.n.]

Page 24. *Let the uninformed reader be aware that among the above-mentioned numbers relationships exist that are called "sonorous." For instance, the hemiolion occurs when the larger of two numbers contains the smaller as well as the latter's half: like 3 in relationship to 2, since both 2 and its half, 1, are contained in 3. The epitriton occurs when of two numbers the larger contains the smaller and the latter's third part, like 4 in relation to 3. There are, in short, conjunctions and disjunctions of microtimes that in Zebulonia can be found in natural elements and in those of the firmament; that is, you have the hemiolion olive tree, the

144

epitriton cloud, the triplar blackbird, the quadruple wind, the epitriton moon. [G.B.]

Page 30. *Mastro is the traditional title given to an accomplished craftsman in Sicily. [Tr.n.]

Page 36. *Michele Amari (Palermo 1806-Florence 1889) is the famous historian of the Arabs in Sicily. His monumental work is *Storia dei Musulmani di Sicilia*, 3 vols. (Florence, 1854-1872). He also wrote an important work on the Sicilian Vespers, *La guerra del Vespro siciliano* (Paris, 1843). [Tr.n.]

Page 47. *Cart panels depicting scenes from the sagas of the French paladins are common in Sicilian folk art. [Tr.n.]

Page 54. *A meter (ἐνόπλιος) employed in warlike poetry, or for a war dance. [Tr.n.]

Page 57. *On Culinary Art.* [Tr.n.]

Page 58. *Children dressed as monks pursuant to a vow made by their parents, usually during an illness of the child, were sometimes sent to live in the nearby monastery for a period of time, where they served chiefly as errand boys for the friars. [Tr.n.]

Page 63. *The name of the Greek colony that is now Agrigento. [Tr.n.]

Page 67. *See my book, *L'enorme tempo* (Milan: Rizzoli, 1976). [G.B.]

Page 69. *According to Diodorus Siculus (vol. V, pp 177-78), these pots were first brought to the island by the Chalcidians and the Corinthians. The small town of Kalàt-Yeròn achieved a particular versatility in crafting them. In the original cylindrical shape with a widening mouth, they were made of unglazed clay as well as clay shiny with glazes over which palm trees, fava beans, birdcatchers and verses by the notary Jacopo da Lentini were reproduced. The noble families used cànteri with twisted bronze or gilded handles. The cloths used to cover the said objects were embellished with filigree work and trapunto roses. [G.B.]

Page 72. *"Fascism? What was that?" someone will ask a hundred years from now. [G.B.]

Page 88. *A well-known late nineteenth-century writer from Mineo. [Tr.n.]

Page 104. *The snakes were used in folk medicine. [Tr.n.]

Page 117. *Bonaviri notes that the Romans were very fond of this little-known plant from Cyrenaica. It belongs to the umbelliferae, or carrot, family; it is a kind of fennel, with a fairly thick stem. In Bonaviri's youth, the stem was also used for corking bottles. [Tr.n.]

Page 140. ˙On this point see Maffeo's manual (Mondadori edition), and *Le mechaniche* by Galileo Galilei (Leyden, 1638), which we have consulted: "It happens that, as a result of the impact of solar and cometary matter, wandering without increment in the great pasture of heaven, against the thin (as it is thought) lunar crust or its craters, parts of these stones break off and fall back to our earth in a furious rush" (p. 27). [G.B.]

*This Book Was Completed on September 12, 1990 at
Italica Press, New York, New York and Was
Set in Galliard. It Was Printed on 50 lb
Glatfelter Natural Acid-Free Paper
with a Smyth-Sewn Binding by
McNaughton & Gunn,
Ann Arbor, MI
U. S. A.*

* *

*